"These stories turn the reader's ... Wheeler spins stunning arabesques, scoring the surface of his characters' reality to reveal the malice, confusion, and ultimate frailty of us all."

—Jonis Agee, author of *The Bones of Paradise*

"Theodore Wheeler's debut collection of fiction *Bad Faith* is a perfect lesson in perfidy, deception, and duplicity, a contemplative exploration of the vagaries of the double-minded human heart."

—Amina Gautier, author of *The Loss of All Lost Things*

"Wheeler's characters occupy the edges of their lives, the gray places of the heart. They yearn for inclusion at the same time that they feel pulled into isolation. At the heart of this brilliant book is the desire to connect—with others, with the world around us, and with the lost parts of ourselves. Filled with powerful insights and a nuanced understanding of human nature, *Bad Faith* is a major achievement, and Theodore Wheeler is a writer to be reckoned with."

—Brent Spencer, author of *Rattlesnake Daddy: A Son's Search for His Father*

"Superbly chiseled prose conveying extraordinarily hardscrabble lives, *Bad Faith* explores dark alleys within the epiphany that some of us are fated to more hell than heaven on earth. Theodore Wheeler is the real deal and then some."

—Mark Wisniewski, author of *Watch Me Go*

# BAD FAITH

THEODORE WHEELER

For Isaac,

Great to meet you!

Best wishes,

[signature]

Berkeley, CA

8/3/16

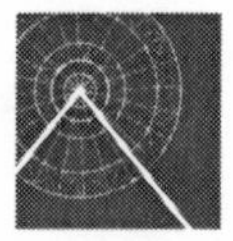

**Queen's Ferry Press**
8622 Naomi Street
Plano, TX 75024
www.queensferrypress.com

The characters and events in this book are fictitious. Any similarity to real persons, living or dead, is entirely coincidental and not intended by the author.

First Edition



Cover illustration by Michael Mihok
Cover design by Brian Mihok
Interior design by Ryan W. Bradley

ISBN 978-1-938466-66-3

Printed in the United States of America

These stories originally appeared in the following publications: "The Mercy Killing of Harry Kleinhardt" in *Midwestern Gothic;* "The Missing" in *The Southern Review;* "How to Die Young in a Nebraska Winter" in *The Kenyon Review;* "Impertinent, Triumphant" on *Five Chapters;* "Violate the Leaves" in *Boulevard;* "The Current State of the Universe" in *The Cincinnati Review;* "Attend the Way" in *Heavy Feather Review;* "Bad Faith" appeared in separate parts as "The First Night of My Down-and-Out Sex Life" in *Confrontation*, "The Man Who Never Was" in *Weekday*, and "On a Train from the Place Called Valentine" in *Boulevard* and *New Stories from the Midwest 2015.* The between-story vignettes appeared collectively as "Kleinhardt's Women" on *Fogged Clarity.*

for Nicole

# Contents

# The Mercy Killing of Harry Kleinhardt

Aaron helped his dad down the steps and through the door of the Congress. He tried to hurry to a booth before they made a scene, his dad weak, barely upright, but the regulars at the bar had already turned to watch them struggle. Harry's weight swayed more and more to Aaron's arm until they got to a booth where Harry could drop into the vinyl and catch his breath. Aaron was breathless too. He wasn't built to take care of people, but this was what he'd come home to do.

That afternoon Harry had received treatment at the county clinic outside town, where an IV dripped toxins into his veins. Harry had colon and lung cancer, and he required a stop at the Congress on the way home from the clinic. Aaron obliged.

"Here," Aaron said, circling back from the bar to clack a gin and soda on the tabletop. Harry didn't look up. He slid the drink under his bowed head to sip the top off.

Harry's skin was damaged but he wasn't an old man, in his middle fifties. His pores gaped and were discolored, his fingertips smooth with burns. Harry was a farmer. He'd worked with chemicals his whole life, fertilizers and pesticides. Nothing was capable of saving Harry now, he knew that. He took the chemo because the county was required to give it.

The Congress was a low-ceiling joint tucked into the side of a motel near the highway in Jackson County. Its patrons were a used-up sort of transgenerational loser. They huddled around dim candles and palmed cocktails. The collars of freebie Marlboro tee shirts lolled around their necks. This was the first time Aaron had been to the Congress, but Harry was known here. Everything in Jackson County was put into context by family—by whose daddy owned what, whose uncle worked where, whose granddaddy died fighting who. These people knew about Aaron because they knew his father.

Aaron left Jackson when he was fifteen, a runaway, and hopped freights to Omaha. He lived on his own a month before he got sent to Boys Town for stealing a car. Harry didn't mind Aaron getting sent away to finish his schooling—he thought the boy might be better off far away. They were so isolated out on the farm. They didn't belong to a church, they weren't on speaking terms with their neighbors. Aaron had showed up at school as little as the county allowed. It wasn't a good situation. Aaron had waited at home most every night, growing up, while Harry was at the Congress. He didn't think anyone would miss him when he ran off. After the state stuck him in Boys Town he didn't hear from anybody in town, except for sporadic phone calls from Harry that only confirmed to Aaron that his presence wasn't necessary at home.

Most people in Jackson had forgotten about Aaron Kleinhardt by the time he came back to help his father die. He was thirty-two. He wore his hair shaggy, like he had in college, so he looked younger. The bangs hung over his eyes.

Among the regulars at the Congress was a guy called Little John. Little John had a crew cut that made a strange frame for his face. There wasn't enough hair to balance his jowls, so his chin looked even fatter than it already was. It was

Little John's presence that perked up Harry. Once he came over to their booth, Harry lifted his head and scowled in an excited, mischievous way. Little John flipped a pack of smokes to the table.

"How do you know him?" Aaron asked.

"I have a blind on your dad's land," Little John explained. "We're buck hunters."

"LJ's a crop adjuster," Harry added. "But he's not too much of an asshole for an insurance man."

"What's your line of work, Harry's boy?"

"I studied history in college," Aaron said. "Plains history."

"You mean like Nebraska?"

"Not exactly. There's plains lots of places."

"He unloads trucks," Harry said. "There's trucks full of shit lots of places too."

Aaron didn't want to explain why he was out of work. He'd been tramping, living with women he met. He glanced around the barroom and grinned dumbly when they talked about work. Aaron didn't know how to explain what it was he did. He sat there and played along, hoping no one asked why someone who claimed to make a living from lifting and moving cargo had such measly arms.

"You live in Omaha?" Little John asked.

"That's right."

"Your dad goes on about it sometimes—how his boy's smarter than the rest of us, if for no other reason than he don't have to live in Jackson County."

Harry snorted at this, like he didn't believe he'd ever brag on his boy. "It don't take smarts to move boxes."

"I doubt that's true." Little John smiled. He waited until Harry closed his eyes again then leaned across the booth to

Aaron. “It’s nice what you’re doing for your dad. It means a lot, you being here to take care of him.”

“It’s nothing.”

“Listen. You’re doing the right thing.”

“It’s an errand,” Aaron said. He refused to explain what he meant.

They drove through town after leaving the Congress, Aaron and Harry, idling in a Chevy Lumina over the red brick streets that surrounded the town square and the Jackson County Courthouse. The courthouse was small, merely two stories high, but Aaron had been in awe when he was a little boy, afraid to even gaze up at its moss-covered spires because the courthouse was such an important building in Jackson. A German preacher was tarred-and-feathered there, a long time ago. The old clock in the tower boomed out the time as they passed. It was four o’clock. There were shops along Main Street for household goods, for insurance, Little John’s name painted across the glass, for rock candy and candles, for baby clothes on consignment. There was an old lumberyard with stacks of boards and plywood housed in slumped, open buildings, all of it enclosed by chain-link fence. At the edge of town was a towering Co-Op silo, plaster white and ominous. Because there was nothing else tall around, the silo swayed when Aaron looked up, the Lumina’s tires humming as they hit county road asphalt. The house was eleven miles outside town.

Harry needed help settling into the mudroom when they got to the farm. Aaron set him up in his chair, its ratty green cover all but gone, then covered his legs with a blanket and spun the dial to Limbaugh.

“I’m fine,” Harry said. “Go leave me alone.”

It was a cool November day, but not cold. Sunlight shined through the storm windows and made the dust in the air swirl. Harry melted into the cushion and closed his eyes. A cigarette burned between his fingers. He could have been asleep but Aaron knew he wasn't. Harry was a reptile warming his skin.

This was the farmhouse Aaron grew up in, a gray cottage near the highway. There was a small bathroom off the kitchen, a yellow blanket that covered the doorway to Harry's bedroom, and the living room where Aaron slept on a cot as a boy. A pull-out sofa was in the living room now, that's where he'd been sleeping. The mudroom was the main venue of the house, where Harry rested and smoked and listened to the radio. Harry used to pull on his rubber waders in the mudroom before going out to work, when he still farmed. He spent most of his time there, sipping drags off cigarettes and gulping gin.

**H**arry moved carefully when he came into the kitchen. His feet slid across the linoleum. He tossed his smokes on top of the refrigerator.

"Sit down," Aaron said. "I'm making dinner."

Harry brushed the newspaper off the table to the floor then needed help easing into his chair, Aaron's hands in his armpits. His mouth was open, his breath phlegm-heavy. "Take it easy," he said. "Don't have to goddamn manhandle me."

Aaron pulled the bread and a couple eggs out of the refrigerator.

"You need to go soon," Harry said. "Nobody asked you to stick around."

"You can't get rid of me. I got a good reason being here."

Aaron couldn't tell if his dad actually wanted him there, but he thought he did. Aaron melted a tab of butter into the pan and waited until scorched dairy hit his nose, his cue to crack the eggs. There were salt and pepper shakers, an old metal spatula, the balancing of bread at the edge of the pan to soften. The rasping whistle of Harry's breath as it cut through the exhaust fan rumble.

It rained and the breeze blew droplets against the window, washing dust off the pane. Aaron watched puddles form in the clay beyond the driveway where red water mixed in a boot print, and farther on still, where rain pelted the empty quonset that used to hold tractors, seeders, and sprayers before his dad was forced to sell his implements and partition his land. Aaron liked cooking for his father, to let the eggs sizzle. Harry wouldn't eat much, but they'd sit together at the table.

"You should go," Harry repeated. "This…" he swept a shaking hand over the table. "This is happening whether you're here or not."

Aaron laid the bread out on saucers. The eggs slid off the spatula like jelly and landed on the toast. From the center of the table Harry pulled a napkin from a box and tried to unfold it in his lap. His fingertips pinched at the napkin to separate its edges.

"Are we going to eat or what?"

**A**aron never actually knew his mother, not in any real way. When he was a boy he fantasized about her coming back to rescue him from Nebraska, to take him with her to L.A., New York, wherever she'd landed. Aaron knew so little about her that these dreams seemed like they could somehow become reality. His dad never told what actually happened to her. If Aaron pestered him enough Harry would say, "She's alive.

That's all you need to know. That woman you like to call your mom is still breathing somewhere."

Aaron didn't learn much about the world outside Jackson County until later, but even as a boy it seemed pretty obvious that things were better elsewhere—and that this was the reason his mother left. There was an old joke about how Jackson was the only county in this Union state to be named after a Confederate general, and that about summed up how out of step Jackson was with the rest of the planet, Aaron thought.

More than likely his mother met a man in Sioux City and took off from there. Maybe a friend of hers had a lead for some quick money, liquor, or drugs, or a chance to work a back room at a horse track. Over the years Aaron convinced himself of a thousand scenarios. She was a nomadic bounty hunter in Texas, a piano teacher in Vienna, an Amazon explorer searching out El Dorado, an African missionary. That she was the wife of an extraordinarily rich man was a recurring theme. They were ridiculous dreams. Aaron didn't have much to work with in creating them.

He had a vague recollection of when she left, of being dropped at a neighbor's one evening for dinner. He was five. His mother drove off with a woman and left him. Aaron ate with the neighbor family. They watched TV. He sat on the floor with a kid his age, between the couch the neighbors sat on and the TV. The kid had a Richard Petty matchbox racing set, but he wouldn't share. The only thing Aaron had with him was a plush stuffed elephant.

Aaron stayed up late that night because his mother was late coming for him. He fell asleep on the floor and at some point the neighbors moved him next to their kid in bed.

Harry was driving trucks overnight then, during the winter, a route between local swine lots and Omaha. The neighbors got ahold of him, but it was morning before he could make it back to town. The neighbor mom was making breakfast, pancakes and eggs, the other kid not yet awake, when Harry pulled his semi into the yard. Aaron forgot his plush elephant there. His dad never talked to the neighbors much, so he never got it back.

Aaron's mother must have slipped the neighbors some money when she dropped him off, $25 or so, which was a lot for watching a kid in those days, or else they wouldn't have taken him. Aaron always wished they hadn't. It seemed like it would have been better if his mother had brought him with her, wherever she went off to. That was when Aaron still believed she was a glamorous type, before Harry threw out her things. A half-bottle of perfume. The water cooler she'd won at the county fair. Her clothes still in the cedar dresser. There were pictures Harry forgot in the storm cellar, though, in a box under some cans of spray paint. Pictures of Harry and her sitting in each others' arms on the hood of an old Dodge, a field of corn behind them, or smiling together in the dim lamplight of some party or another.

**A**aron drove around after Harry fell asleep that evening—on brick-paved streets and asphalt county roads, on the gravel access spurs between fallow fields. There wasn't much else to do if he didn't want to be at home or sit in that dreary bar. He'd return home later to the sofa bed and listen to his dad's breathing from the other room.

Aaron was driving his dad's car because he didn't have one of his own. There were other ways of traveling. Aaron was an expert at distance walking and hitchhiking and hopping trains and stealing cars. It was easy for him to get around if he had a purpose. He'd hitched to Jackson County this time, but would drive the Lumina while he was here.

Most nights he just parked on a country road between the windbreaks. A gun sat next to him on the seat. It was nothing special, a small pistol, nickel-plated with a handle of hard black rubber. He kept it in his messenger bag, along with the other things he needed. His wallet and ID, a stick of deodorant, a change of underwear. Things that belonged to other people too. A wedding band. A locket with two thumbnail photographs inside. An infant's sock.

His camera was in the bag. Aaron won the camera a couple years before, betting on college football in a Lincoln barroom. He never would have guessed how much he'd come to depend on the thing. It was a small digital camera, blue and silver, and fit in the palm of his hand. Aaron used the camera to pick up women—saying he'd like to snap a picture of one as an excuse to call her pretty. It was an old bit, one that almost always worked. He was small and skinny, and for reasons he never really understood, women trusted him. He found that most of them would do what he asked if he was persistent enough.

They went to the bank the next morning. Harry wanted to deposit some coins he'd saved in a coffee can, something he'd always called Aaron's college fund. It was a joke only Harry was in on. Even though Aaron had gone to college, he'd never seen a dime from the coffee can.

A woman and her two boys were ahead of them in line. The boys were toddlers and held to their mom's legs, each pinching the panty hose that stretched below her hemline. They stared at Harry's scars, the way he winced while standing, the dead skin that stuck out through his short hair, and the open sores on his neck. Harry wore a pin on his coat that said *Cancer Sucks*.

Aaron watched the teller in the cage at the front of the line. She must have been new in town, she didn't look like the other county women, young, with a dark complexion and greasy black hair. She was dumpy in a way that Aaron could tell she drank too much—the thickness of flesh around her cheeks and neck, hollows below her eyes. When they got to the counter, she explained that the bank didn't accept loose change like Harry wanted to give.

"I'm sorry," she said. "We don't even have the machine anymore. But you can take some papers if you want to roll them yourself at home. How's that sound?"

Aaron started to say that it wasn't a big deal, but Harry interrupted him.

"What's she saying?" he asked, pushing Aaron out of the way. "Won't they do it?"

"I'm sorry," the teller said. "Is there anything else we can do?" She explained again about the machine being gone. Harry slammed his hands on the counter to stop her. It was frightening how a man so decrepit could make such noise.

"Don't do me any favors. Just deposit the money. This is your business, isn't it? Isn't this a bank?"

"I'm sorry. I'll get in trouble."

"Don't say that again. Okay? Don't tell me you're sorry, bitch, because we both know what that's worth."

The bank manager rushed to see what the problem was. "Can I help you?" he said, shielding the girl. Harry still glowered at her when she backed away, even as he struggled to catch his breath, as his body deflated to its diseased state.

Aaron had forgotten what it was like to stand there helpless when his dad went off. He was associated with the man. He was the one person in the world who was inexorably tied to Harry Kleinhardt.

"Why do you do that?" he asked later, alone with him in the car.

"What are you talking about?"

"Treating people like that. That's what I mean. Like you treated the girl."

Harry wheezed out a laugh, hunched into the bench seat of his Lumina. "Those people don't care about you. They certainly don't give a shit about me."

"What's accomplished though? What can you gain by —?"

"Nothing," Harry said. "It's not supposed to do nothing. There isn't one damn thing I'd trade for what they got. People like that don't understand and it pisses me off."

There was tapping on the roof of the mudroom, the first sleet of the season, Thanksgiving week.

Harry had been in the mudroom a long time and Limbaugh was over. The station was playing country-western music. Behind him, in the window, the atmospheric dust settled in the western sky, burning red and orange in the last sunlight. Aaron knocked on the doorframe to let Harry know dinner was about ready, fried bologna this time, but Harry didn't move. He'd been smoking in the mudroom with his waders on. The cold ash of a cigarette hung from his lips. His face had gone slack and stiff, his eyes rest shut. His hands were in half fists on the bulge of his coat.

Aaron stopped in the doorway. When he touched his dad's cheek the cigarette ash collapsed onto Harry's chin.

"Is it—?" Aaron said. He kneeled into the cushion and whispered within the sleet on the rooftop.

Suddenly there was beeping from the kitchen. The smoke alarm going off. Aaron jumped at the noise but didn't move away from Harry. "Are you here?" he asked. He put his ear next to his dad's nose.

"What's the racket?" Harry shouted. He jerked back from Aaron, arms raised, and knocked his head against the drywall. "What are you doing to me?"

The pan handle scalded Aaron's hand when he grabbed it, but there wasn't a fire. It was just the bologna that set off the alarm, the bottom burned black. Aaron tossed the mess in the trash then cooled his fingers under the faucet. He offered to make something else but Harry told him not to. "It wouldn't be any use if you did."

Aaron didn't know what to do with himself. He made a sandwich and ate it. He paced inside the house, in the two rooms, and packed his suitcase. He decided to go into town, to the Congress, and that's what he told Harry as he walked out through the mudroom to the car.

The Congress was busy, ninety minutes into happy hour. Groups of men talked loudly, a few couples danced, lines formed outside the bathrooms. The top pages of a hot-rod magazine curled off from a stack at the end of the bar.

She was alone. He recognized her. "You're the teller from the bank, aren't you?"

"My name's Emily," the girl said. She didn't seem to mind when Aaron hung his messenger bag over the stool back next to her.

"I'm sorry about what happened. He shouldn't talk to you like that."

"It's okay." She spun a straw in her drink. "We know all about Harry Kleinhardt."

"Do you?" Aaron said.

He fixed his eyes on different parts of her face until laughter bubbled up out of her nerves. He laughed too and turned away to take a breath. The air was hotter here than it had been earlier that week, the music louder. The neon lights bled brighter. The walls were lined with old men waiting out their liquor, but there were handfuls of young men too. At the other end of the bar were a few women in tight Wranglers, braless under plaid button-downs. Eager men surrounded these few women.

"Let me buy you a drink," Aaron said. "It's the least I can do. Consider it compensation for the aggravation my father causes."

The girl leaned down when she talked to Aaron, showed some cleavage from inside her bank-issued polo, unbuttoned as far as it would go to flash the freckles of her chest. She wore a padded pink bra, her bitties loose inside it.

"Are you really his kid?" she asked.

Aaron nodded.

"I never thought about Harry Kleinhardt having any family." She glanced at Aaron like she still might not believe it.

"What are you doing here?" she asked. "Just back for Thanksgiving?"

"I don't think you want to know that." Aaron guided his bangs to the side of his forehead and smiled at her.

"Come on," she said. "I'm game. You can tell me and I won't repeat it."

"You wouldn't tell anyone."

"Tell me the truth. Why are you here?"

Aaron didn't answer for a long time. Emily tried turning away, but she couldn't stop looking at him while he was looking at her, while he was smiling. His hand found its way to her thigh and she let it stay.

"Do I need an excuse to visit Jackson County?" he asked. "Isn't the Congress enough?"

She shook her head.

"This place is the worst. Don't you know that? This is where the lowlifes come when they're up to no good. Where airheads come to get laid."

"We wouldn't want to be like them, would we?"

"No, we wouldn't. This place stinks."

Emily pulled a cigarette from her purse and lit it, puckering her lips as she exhaled. Her hair was pulled back. Black curls snuck around her neck. She had a small chin and her face appeared to flare out as it approached the hairline.

"You know," Aaron said, "you're really a pretty girl."

"I doubt that."

"I mean it. Would it be too much to take a photograph?"

"What do you mean? You and me take a picture together?"

"Of course," Aaron said. He fingered the strap of his bag, ready to pull out his camera and snap a shot of her.

"You can't take it here," she objected. "Who in the world would want to be remembered like this?"

"Come on. Just one. Indulge me."

"No," she said, loud enough for Aaron to concede.

"Okay," he said, his feelings hurt. "But we'll snap one later. Promise me that."

"Sure," the girl said. "We'll drink a few Long Islands and then take a nice portrait for the Christmas card."

Aaron heard Emily laughing after he excused himself to the bathroom. A few of the other men at the bar joined her too. "Christmas card!"

"You're too much, Em. You know that?"

Mangy green carpet covered the floor of the Congress, except in the men's room, where someone had torn it out. The floor was sticky and wet. At the urinal, Aaron noticed a shirt button in the filter. The bathroom was tiny, a small cinderblock cell, a dripping sink on the wall between the urinal and toilet. There were no dividers, no stalls, just two kinds of toilets, three in a pinch, on the other side of a punched-through black door.

Later in the night, Emily would apologize for making fun of Aaron wanting to take that picture of her. All the other people in the bar laughed long and hard at how she'd put him down. She was sorry for that, even though Aaron kept smiling the whole time. He never let on what he was thinking. The way anger seethed inside his heart. How all he could want then was to make her regret laughing at him.

They were driving the brick roads around town when she apologized. They circled the town square and the courthouse, its moss-covered spires. There was the slumping old lumberyard, the ghostly Co-Op silo gray in the darkness. She suggested they stop. "I live around here. You can take that picture if you want."

She had a small white house close to the school. Aaron parked in the driveway and they went inside.

**H**arry was still in the mudroom, his eyes closed.

It was almost morning. Mist gathered on the windshield as Aaron pulled off the road. He left the car door open when he stopped. It dinged to tell him this, the dome light spreading over the yard.

Aaron stood outside the storm door to watch his dad sleep, the lit-up car behind him. The flap of his messenger bag was open, resting on the small of his back.

Harry's favorite memory was watching Aaron sleep when he was a baby. Aaron thought of this, a story Harry told all the time when Aaron was growing up. "It made me realize my luck," Harry would say. "You breathing in fits. My hand on your chest just to make sure. You really did look like me. The ears. The cowlick. Your eyes."

Harry's eyes twitched open at the noise when it happened. Then his jaw dropped, the blanket fell from his knees. One of his eyes wouldn't close and stared past Aaron.

The storm door latched, Aaron's hand on the handle as he looked back at his dad in the mudroom one last time. He told himself that he should leave, and again, that he needed to go. There was a cold whispering mist, so fine in its composition, that unless you were standing in it with him, you wouldn't even know it was there.

He noticed how she watched him circle the plaza fountain. Her head tilted skyward, as if she wanted him to think she didn't notice. He was aware of her glances. She sipped cola when she looked. She peeked beyond the curve of a plastic bottle.

He circled twice, hesitating when he was on her side of the fountain to bring the stub of a cigarette to his lips, his head raised over chattering students on their way to class. Smoke drifted from his mouth as he peered dumb at the names stamped on distant buildings. He shook his head then circled the fountain again, patted the pockets of his jean jacket like he'd lost something. A green messenger bag hung off his shoulder.

She watched breathlessly the third time he circled toward her, when he was holding it out in front of himself. She leaned forward on her bench to look, forgetting to be inconspicuous because he'd been swallowed in a crowd. He stepped clumsily in front of bicycles and edged between groups of women in conversation. Then he bent to look at it. It was a ring. He lifted it in the sunlight when he knew she was watching, a wedding band that would look familiar to anyone, in the thickness of the metal, in the way the silver glinted in the light.

He made his way to her and grinned pathetically, searching the faces of others before picking her out—her, of course. She looked stunned when he smiled at her. The ring was between his fingers but he slid it into his jeans before speaking. Her eyes followed somewhat desperately as the band disappeared into his fob pocket.

"Excuse me," he said. He pulled a digital camera from his messenger bag. "Do you mind if I take your picture?"

This is how it started with Jessica Harding.

He told her to call him Aaron.

# The Missing

Worthy told Steve to come visit San Sal for a few days. Why San Sal? Because I live in San Sal, Worthy told him.

Worthy told Steve what airline to fly. United. And where to connect. Houston. Worthy told him to forget his Delta miles, forget Atlanta. Take United. Go through Houston.

Worthy told Steve wild stories about El Salvador. Bus rides up chuckholed alleys into ghettos where even police were afraid to go because gangs controlled that territory; that San Salvador was the murder capital of the world, no matter what claims were made by Kabul or Baghdad or Tegucigalpa. Worthy talked about getting drunk on something called coco loco. And girls dancing in clubs where the Salvadoran Geddy Lee played bass with one hand and keys with the other. And girls dancing in clubs who were on the hunt for American men, for the green card, but were often left behind in San Salvador if pregnant, and there was little recourse for a woman of that kind. Over the phone Worthy told him about girls dancing in a nudie bar called Lips that had a taco bar next door that was also called Lips. Worthy was persuasive. Even the plastic bags filled with soft, slimy cheese called queso fresco that Worthy bought on the street, even that sounded attractive when Worthy talked about it. Even when the Mrs.

grabbed the phone and told Worthy that if anything bad happened to Steve she'd know who to hold responsible.

Do you understand? the Mrs. told Worthy. If he doesn't come back, I will come down there and fuck you up.

The Mrs. told Steve about all the reasons why it was stupid to go. He had a family to think about. I'm six months pregnant, the Mrs. told him.

You'll do what you want anyway, the Mrs. told him, but at least try and be smart about it. What's it prove going there for a long weekend? Isn't there enough to worry about here?

You don't belong in El Salvador, the Mrs. told him.

That's why Steve had to go.

Worthy told him to look for a Subaru Outback at the airport after he cleared customs. He was supposed to tell customs that he was staying at the apartment complex where Worthy lived with other doctors, where foreign diplomats lived. But the customs agent at the airport had never heard of Dr. Worthy. The customs agent wanted to be told an address. The name of a hotel. Steve had nothing to tell the customs agent. Worthy hadn't passed on this information. All Steve could do was hand over his passport and shrug. He didn't speak Spanish and was in the wrong line because the gringo line was backed up with missionaries from Evansville and Dallas–Fort Worth. The customs agent's supervisor came over. She wore a yellow blazer that was big on her.

My friend Worthy is coming to pick me up, Steve told the supervisor. I'm going to stay at his apartment. In San Sal.

The customs agent and the supervisor discussed between themselves and agreed it was fine for Steve to enter. This is you, they told him, pointing to his passport, to the photo he'd taken nine years before, when his skin was smoother, his hair thicker, his chin more distinctly there. He had ten dollars American to buy a visa. That was good enough.

That's how it goes, Worthy told him once he was outside the airport and buckled up in Worthy's Subaru Outback and the air conditioning was blowing.

Sometimes they don't ask where you're going, Worthy told him. They just want the ten.

Once they got to the apartment, Worthy told Steve they'd go to the mountains the next day.

In the morning they drove out into the country.

They burn their garbage, Worthy said to explain the smell, thumbing out the window at smoggy fires shack-dwelling locals tended near the road.

It did smell bad. Steve thought it smelled like the trash can he put dirty diapers in at home. Like the shit of an eight-month-old.

Worthy drove to the mountains. They went to Ataco because there was a shrine there on top of a mountain, a mountain you could hike up, up a shady path where men wielding machetes moved in the leaves, where men worked a coffee plantation with machetes and canteens filled with yerba maté. In the cobblestone alleys of Ataco a nightclub called Portland served Cuban club sandwiches and Suprema beer for lunch. Steve had visited Worthy a few times in Portland, the one in Oregon, where Worthy did a surgical residency years before. They'd gone to Tube and to Shanghai Tunnel, where fresh citrus was squeezed for whiskey cocktails. Maybe there was more to the real Portland than Cuban sandwiches and Salvadoran beer and "Gangnam Style" on the PA, like was played twice during lunch in the nightclub Portland, but Steve didn't care.

After lunch Worthy scouted for a room that would be needed for the following weekend, to return to with a Peace Corps girl who would put out if meals and a hot shower were involved.

Worthy drove them to Juayúa. They paid respects to the Black Jesus shrine in the white stone cathedral in Juayúa. Worthy told Steve they should get a tuk tuk to take up the side of the mountain to see the falls.

Los Chorros de la Calera, Worthy told him. That's what it's called.

The boy next to the tuk tuk didn't say anything. The boy didn't know English. The boy didn't appear to know Spanish. Worthy talked to the boy's father. The boy's father was the driver. The driver said he'd take them to the waterfalls. Upside the mountain. The driver set a low price and Worthy told the driver that would be fine. This was November and not much was going on. Worthy paid half up-front, then they all squeezed into the rusty three-wheeled taxi—two big Americans in the back with the boy between them on the metal bench seat. Both Steve and Worthy craned their heads toward the middle, over the boy's head, so they'd all fit.

The driver scooted them around the square in Juayúa. Women set up card tables to sell pirated DVDs and CDs and salted fruit and packaged marzipan. The tuk tuk rattled and shook. The mountain path was washed out, rutted through. The driver, one hand on the wheel, the other on the throttle to rev and unrev, kept the motor going through its pops and sputters. The boy laughed between Worthy and Steve in the back.

The driver stopped halfway up the mountain, where the path ended at a chain-link fence. They got out. Worthy told the driver to wait.

Waterfalls rumbled somewhere beyond the gate, beyond the wall of leaves and spindly tropical trees that quivered up to sunlight. Steve followed Worthy to the noise, along a footpath that went into the jungle.

Steve thought they'd be alone at the falls for some reason, but there were people, backpackers, a girl in a blue bikini swimming in the basin pool where the smaller of the falls stopped, before a bigger one cascaded to the bottom of the valley.

Worthy told him to not swim in the water.

It's freezing. That water comes from the top. Jump into icy water like that and your heart might stop. An old guy like you, Worthy joked.

Backpackers swam and splashed and yelled about how cold the water was. One of the backpackers hauled up onto a stone ledge with a hanging vine then leapt back, hollering, into the water. Aside from the girl in the blue bikini, only young men swam in the basin pool. Their packs leaned together, away from the cliff. Their clothes trailed to the water. The girl in the blue bikini was very blond. Maybe she's German, Steve thought. He saw the girl's body under the icy-clear mountain water. The girl's long arms and legs shivered like a mirage under the waves she made with her kicking and paddling and laughter.

Worthy shouted Ahoy! to the girl and the backpackers. How is it in there?

One of the backpackers told Worthy the water was fine.

Going to join us? the girl in the blue bikini asked.

Still thinking, Worthy told her.

Worthy stood at the edge of a narrow crevasse. The crevasse was a few feet across but a long way down. A wooden stepladder lay over the gap. Worthy walked across the stepladder to tell the girl in the blue bikini about being a doctor on a humanitarian mission. Worthy explained how a consortium of Evangelical churches in Allen, Texas, paid physicians to move here, to work here, to live in an apartment complex in San Salvador, an apartment complex with armed guards, balconies off the bedrooms, a swimming pool and BBQ pit, yes, communal amenities of the apartment complex the Evangelicals paid for. You should see it sometime, Worthy said. It's nice.

Steve crawled over the horizontal ladder to the basin pool, next to Worthy. Steve didn't stand after he crossed. He sat with his legs splayed, not too close to the edge. When he looked down there was nothing until the bottom. The bottom stubbled with trees, hundreds of feet down, thousands. Steve didn't know much about distances. What sounded accurate to people who knew such things, what didn't. The measurement of distances didn't really matter to him. You wouldn't want to fall, he told himself. That's what mattered.

Steve thought about what people told him back home. The doctor, in particular, his wife's doctor, he should say, the ob-gyn, had told him not to worry. He and the Mrs. went through a lot the last time they'd had a baby, not even a year ago, and now they were going to have a third, an Irish twin. People had told him the Mrs. couldn't get pregnant while she was nursing. What people had told him was wrong. It will all work out in the end, the ob-gyn had told him, like the last time. Steve and the Mrs. were lucky, they already had two healthy girls. But what they'd gone through when daughter two was born, that's what he worried about. The blue spells in the delivery room. The specially made neonatal oxygen mask. The NICU. That other doctor, daughter two's doctor, he should say, with a mustache and coffee mug and blue pinstriped dress shirt, the crisp, starched, pressed white coat. That other doctor told them the baby needed a spinal tap, when they were in the NICU. Is that okay, that other doctor told them. They didn't answer. It wasn't a question. That other doctor asked the Mrs. if she smoked cigarettes during the pregnancy. If the Mrs. drank alcohol, took pills, smoked marijuana—that could be the problem, and why the baby couldn't breathe right. That other doctor asked the Mrs. if she snorted cocaine while the baby was inside her. The Mrs. cried. The Mrs. hadn't cried yet that morning, not during the baby's blue spell, not when the nurse slapped a button on the wall to call a code, not when all staff on the floor rushed in to shout out what was wrong, the baby not breathing, suddenly, when they took the baby away, the baby blue. Steve had cried. He couldn't stop crying. But the Mrs. didn't cry then because the Mrs. was on drugs, drugs her ob gave her: muscle relaxers, stool softeners, Zofran, Demoral, Pitocin, ibuprofen, the epidural cocktail, which was why the Mrs. was in a wheelchair when that other doctor asked her rude things, when that other doctor told how it would probably be okay, once they got the results from the spinal tap back.

That other doctor was right. It was okay. Daughter two didn't die. Daughter two learned how to breathe in a few days, and they took her home to begin the business of forgetting about blue spells.

The girl in the blue bikini told Steve how she wasn't German like he thought she was. I am Finnish, the girl in the blue bikini said. My name is Anja.

The backpackers told Anja they were leaving. They were backpacking down to the village to get there before sunset. They wanted hand-patted pupusa. They wanted cerveza.

Anja told the backpackers to go on without her. Anja told them she was staying with Worthy.

I just met them guys two days ago, Anja told Worthy and Steve, sweeping her long, Finnish-blond hair around her neck. Her dripping-wet hair.

After they puzzled arms and legs in the tuk tuk—the boy on Steve's lap because Anja was on Worthy's lap—the driver told them the tuk tuk wouldn't start. The driver turned the key but the tuk tuk motor didn't catch.

Worthy didn't know a thing about tuk tuk motors but was willing to take a look.

Worthy couldn't fix the tuk tuk motor.

It was getting close to sunset, Steve thought, or maybe not. How the sunset worked here was a mystery. If it would go dark slowly or all at once. It felt much later than it did before, before the tuk tuk motor didn't catch.

The driver told them there was family nearby. A cousin.

They're all cousins, Worthy told Anja. Worthy circulated these mountains frequently for work. Worthy knew. Worthy tended to locals for osteoporosis, typhoid, juvenile anemia, maladies of the teeth, broken bones, infections of the feet and gums, suicide, rickets, toxic exposure, diarrhea, battery associative of sexual violence, battery associative of alcoholism, juvenile malnutrition, late-onset obesity, rabies, dengue. Worthy was comfortable in the mountain jungle, with the people who lived here and their complaints. Worthy wasn't worried.

They pushed the tuk tuk down the mountain a ways. There were shack houses along the path, sided by two-by-six boards with cracks between each edge so Steve could see in a little. The driver told them they could stay the night. Or they could walk down the path. It was about an hour's walk, the driver told Worthy and Anja, who both spoke Spanish.

We're going to stay here, Worthy said.

It's still light out, Steve told Worthy. We should walk.

Anja took Worthy's hand. Anja leaned into Worthy. Let's wait till morning, Anja said.

Anja told the woman who ran things inside the shack house that she and Worthy would be happy to help with dinner. Anja and Worthy grabbed Tupperware containers and went off for water.

Steve was left behind. He knew Worthy and Anja didn't want him along. He sat in a corner to wait, with some coconut shells, with a stack of VCRs that apparently didn't work and one that did, which was connected to a television. The woman who ran things told Steve something he couldn't understand. An old-timer was there, the woman's husband or father, he guessed. The driver and the boy were there too. The driver told Steve something and pointed to the tuk tuk. The tuk tuk waited outside for the guy who knew how to fix things to come.

Steve wanted to call the Mrs. but couldn't while he was in the mountains. There wasn't cell reception. There wasn't Wi-Fi. He couldn't Skype with the Mrs. That's why he wanted to walk back to Juayúa and get in Worthy's Subaru Outback and go back to Worthy's apartment in San Salvador. Worthy's apartment had Wi-Fi. The Mrs. wouldn't be pleased if they didn't Skype. Steve's two daughters wouldn't be pleased—they'd get no phone-daddy that day, which is what daughter one called him when he was away on business, when she only saw him on Skype, maybe once a day, when there was time to step away from steak and/or sushi business dinners, or slip out of a meeting to video chat with the Mrs. and his daughters back in Milwaukee, which is where they lived. He felt bad he couldn't Skype. He wasn't too pleased with himself, sitting in the shack house with the woman who ran things and the old-timer and the driver and the boy.

The woman who ran things went outside and shouted down the path. Steve didn't know who was coming up the road, who the woman was yelling to. Ya viene, the woman told him, on her way back to the other room. A neighbor came inside the shack house after the woman.

She said to come talk to you, the neighbor said.

Why? Steve asked the neighbor.

I speak English, the neighbor told him, which he'd noticed already. I used to live in the U.S., in L.A.

The neighbor had a chance to speak English with tourists who came through, but the neighbor didn't do this very often. This was embarrassing for the neighbor. The neighbor had been deported from the U.S.

Usually tourists don't stop by for dinner, the neighbor said. Why do you stop for dinner?

There's a girl, Steve told the neighbor.

The neighbor nodded. I saw her. Blue bikini. Tall blonde.

The neighbor's neck and arms were covered with tattoos. MS, the neck tattoos showed in Old English script. Mara Salvatrucha. 13. The neighbor wasn't wearing a shirt. The neighbor had chest tattoos of two women. The women were topless, and each topless woman shared one of the neighbor's nipples. One real nipple for each woman. One nipple for each woman in ink.

The neighbor was short but well-muscled, thirty-five or so, maybe younger. The neighbor looked around the shack house. The neighbor's eyes were dark; there was a softness in them. The neighbor explained the woman who ran things in the shack house was his aunt.

Nobody knows what to do with me, the nephew said, since I came from L.A.

Were you in San Sal before? Steve asked the nephew. Or are you from here?

I was born here, the nephew told him. I went to San Salvador after L.A.

Steve was afraid of the nephew and the nephew's tattoos. Maybe the nephew would kill him. Maybe this was his time. On the United flight from Houston Steve had prepared himself to get mugged while in El Salvador, for his digital camera or his Droid with the Skype app to be stolen. If he went into the mountains, like he was now, he'd get blown away, execution style, and dumped in the trees. Maybe the nephew was too nice a guy for that, Steve hoped. Maybe the nephew was no longer a gang member, no longer a deportee.

Could a person stop being these things? he wondered. Could the nephew just be a nephew? The nephew had tattoos. The nephew had been deported.

There was trouble in the city, the nephew told him. A misunderstanding. In Santa Tecla. Do you know where that is?

Steve told the nephew that he didn't know where Santa Tecla was, or what that meant. It wasn't in L.A., like he thought they were talking about. Santa Tecla was on the outskirts of San Salvador. The nephew returned to the mountains after the misunderstanding. The nephew's aunt took care of things after that. She got her nephew a job in Juayúa sweeping out the cathedral where the shrine to the Black Jesus was. She got her nephew a job spraying off the sticky floors of nightclubs with a hose. She got her nephew a job bagging groceries at a supermarket. She got her nephew a job frying chicken at Pollo Campero. She got her nephew a job repairing the highway. Hooligans put big rocks in the mountain highways, on the bends, so cars would hit the big rocks before they could slow down, which the hooligans found funny. The aunt got the nephew a job removing rocks from the highway.

The aunt brought coffee and stayed close to watch until Steve and the nephew drank from the glasses of coffee.

Steve wondered what the aunt's story was. The old-timer was her father-in-law, the nephew explained. The driver, her brother-in-law. Her husband had been killed in the war, slain by a Salvadoran battalion trained at the School of the Americas, in an ambush, they think, in the slaughter at Tenango y Guadalupe. The aunt and the nephew went to the capital a few years later to look for her husband's portrait in a book of the missing. Human rights groups put together binders filled with portraits of the dead. Guerillas, combatants, the disappeared. The dead from torture, dumped outside the capital for human rights groups to photograph or sketch in graphite.

The nephew was arrested in the capital when the aunt went to look through a book of the missing. The nephew was from a place rebels were from. The nephew was deported from El Salvador, went to L.A., joined a Salvadoran gang in L.A., was deported from L.A., went to El Salvador.

The old-timer was at Tenango y Guadalupe too, the nephew told him, but the old-timer escaped the slaughter.

The old-timer sat in a corner. The old-timer's beard was cut through by a white scar where a bullet crossed his skin at Tenango y Guadalupe.

The aunt banged dishes in the other room, where the sink was. The nephew told him how these things weren't talked about in the shack house. It was true, Steve could see this. The old-timer shifted with displeasure each time the nephew said the words Tenango y Guadalupe.

My name is Ernesto, the nephew said. My name is Steve, he told the nephew.

Ernesto asked where Steve came from.

I live in Wisconsin.

He told Ernesto about his job, about communications management, about how he'd grown up the son of a lumberyard manager in Geneva, Nebraska, where there was a municipal swimming pool filled with blue water in the summertime and cornfields where he caught toads and other toad-like amphibians when he was a boy, and how he went to L.A. a lot for his job now.

Probably a different L.A., Steve said. He stopped midsentence because both knew it was a different L.A. than the one Ernesto had lived in after being deported from El Salvador as a boy.

He told Ernesto about his daughters because that's what he talked about when he thought people were judging him harshly. He talked about his daughters, the first and the second, and how there was going to be a third soon, if everything went okay.

You have a family in Milwaukee, Ernesto said. What are you doing here?

I don't know, he told Ernesto. This is a strange place to end up.

They laughed about that. The old-timer, the driver, the boy. They laughed too.

You know, Steve said. My wife made me promise I wouldn't get myself killed, or else she wouldn't let me come to El Salvador in the first place. Now I'm stuck here on a mountain and can't call her. There's no signal. What do you think she's thinking?

She thinks you're dead, Ernesto told him.

**W**orthy and Anja glowed red-faced and sweaty when they emerged from the trees. Worthy and Anja held hands. Worthy and Anja smiled dumbly to each other.

Worthy told the aunt that there wasn't much water. The water Worthy and Anja brought back from the trees had mostly spilled from the Tupperware they were given.

At dinner Worthy told stories about college. How they met at Marquette. Steve didn't understand a word of the stories until Worthy said Marquette and pointed at him and the room laughed. Worthy had been pre-med, a walk-on guard for the Golden Eagles squad that made the Final Four. Worthy liked talking about being Dwyane Wade's backup, which was true enough for Worthy's purposes. That was over a decade ago. Worthy had curly blond hair and a dark complexion. Worthy's hair had mushroomed into a Jewfro when Worthy backed up Dwyane Wade.

Worthy explained how, these days, the missionaries from Allen, Texas, sent doctors into the mountains to inoculate and educate and leave behind booklets about Protestant heaven. Was it all that great of a gig? Sure it was. There was travel. Worthy helped folks who probably needed help. Maybe Worthy had never dreamed of living in Central America. Worthy sure hadn't during med school, or during the residency in Portland. Worthy wanted to be a surgeon. That didn't work out. But Worthy didn't like to talk about anything that might emit a tangent of failure. The job brought Worthy to El Salvador. Worthy was happy here. Worthy belonged here, pushing through the jungle, parking a Subaru Outback on the cobblestone streets of Juayúa.

The Worthy from college was easy to remember. The Worthy from med school. Worthy belonged to nobody in particular. Worthy belonged everywhere.

Worthy charmed the room. Worthy still wore the same hairstyle he had in college, the blond Jewfro. Worthy passed out dollars to the boy and other kids who snuck in to see what was going on. Worthy fed dollars through the cracks in the shack house's siding to kids outside who were too shy to barge in. Anja said Worthy was like an ATM.

Worthy and Ernesto talked about fútbol they'd seen in Estadio Cuscatlán and Los Dodgers they'd seen in Chavez Ravine. Worthy checked over the teeth and aches and pains of the old-timer. More old-timers came to have their teeth and aches and pains checked over since Worthy had bragged loud enough about being a doctor.

In the morning the guy who knew how to fix things came to fix the tuk tuk. The guy who knew how to fix things found it easy to fix the tuk tuk. The carburetor was dry, the line from the gas tank pinched from being parked too long on an uneven surface.

Worthy told Anja she should come to San Sal. They'd go to Costa del Sol. I belong to the beach club there, Worthy told them. Anja agreed that the beach sounded like fun so they left Juayúa together.

On the ride back from the mountains Steve remembered something else about Worthy. Worthy had called when daughter two was in the NICU, to make it understood that friends were pulling for the Mrs. and Steve and their little angels. It was late at night, Worthy's voice patched in over some satellite linkup that was only for emergencies. Steve was such a mess when Worthy called. The Mrs. was still at the hospital because she wouldn't leave daughter two's side, not while daughter two was in the NICU; daughter two with the special neonatal breathing mask, the blipping monitors that freaked out in the middle of the night when daughter two's oxygen levels inexplicably, persistently, fell. Steve couldn't take being at the hospital. He went back to the house in the afternoon, picked up daughter one from Montessori, made her buttered noodles for dinner, made her cookies and milk, put daughter one in the bathtub, tucked her in with her Clarabelle doll, read *Madeline and the Bad Hat* kneeling at the side of her bed. They prayed together to a cloudy sky; a cloudy sky being how daughter one conceived of God. He answered work e-mails from the couch after daughter one fell asleep, until late. E-mails from HR, his replies explaining that no, he wouldn't miss more work than he had sick time for; that yes, he would cover his responsibilities. Steve had wanted to quit over HR asking that. He'd wanted to smoke cigarettes on the back deck, from a three-year-old pack he kept in a ziplock bag at the bottom of the deep freeze in the basement.

Before Steve went to dig up the emergency cigarettes, Worthy called to check on him.

Steve didn't know what to say to Worthy over the phone. He was brain-dead. Exhausted. He didn't have enough love to give. This he knew. He wasn't smart enough. He wasn't capable when it came to meaningful things. His baby was in the NICU. His baby was breathing, or she was not.

Worthy told him everything would work out. Worthy told him sometimes an infant takes fluid into the lungs while in the womb and has trouble breathing and the infant must clear the fluid by herself.

Mortality is a strange thing, Worthy told Steve. You can put your wife in the best hospital in the world and the same thing would happen. The NICU doc will say the same stuff that yours told you, and then they'll wait to see if the fluid clears. The same as if she was born in a war zone. Or a coffee plantation nowhere close to a clinic.

I don't know if that makes you feel better, Worthy told him, but it's the truth.

They got stuck in traffic in San Sal, on the way to Costa del Sol. Anja with her legs crossed in the front seat next to

Worthy. Worthy said there was an FMLN rally at Estadio Cuscatlán. They'd seen the leftists, the farmers and machete men from plantations, coming in from the countryside, from the mountains. The back of every oil-burning pickup filled with young men. Which was normal anyway.

Anja told them what she knew about the war in El Salvador. Part of a poem from memory, something an American wrote. *The colonel pushed himself from the table. My friend said to me with his eyes: say nothing.*

They ate ceviche at Costa del Sol. They drank coco loco. They stayed at Costa del Sol until sunset and Steve drank cervezas in the Subaru on the way back to San Salvador. In the morning Worthy would drive him to the airport and he'd go home.

I have to piss, Steve told Worthy. Worthy stopped the Subaru at a gas station outside the city. The gas station didn't have a restroom.

Steve went to piss behind the gas station, into the weeds and tall yellowing grass by the edge of a ravine. From the edge of the ravine he could see the orange twinkling lights of San Salvador and the valley.

The young man with a shotgun snuck up behind him. The young man with a shotgun told Steve something in a quiet voice that made Steve jump at how quiet it was, that it came from nowhere at first, then the young man with a shotgun was saying it again.

Short with shaggy hair, the young man, shotgun shells snug in the cartridge loops of his khaki shirt.

Steve didn't know what the young man with a shotgun told him. He stood there and said nothing back, his belt undone, his dick out. The young man pointed to his dick with the shotgun and then to the ravine edge.

The kid's a guard, Worthy told him, leaning out of the Subaru. A friendly. Gas stations have guards. The guard says, Go piss.

Steve heard Worthy and Anja and the guard laughing as he stepped into the yellowing grass at the edge of the ravine. He pissed and had no problem pissing. Let them watch. Let them laugh. He was going home.

Elisabeth Hindmarsh lived on the second floor of a partitioned Victorian in Lincoln. There was an inside stairway to get to her door. Aaron walked in off the street, late at night, but she didn't care. It was after a party and he was going to help her finish the gin.

It was a tiny place. A living room, a kitchenette, a bathroom with black and white checkerboard tile. Red paper lanterns hung on wires sheathed in cloth insulators. Elisabeth was thick-bodied, athletic, her hair dyed a bluish shade of black. She wore a dress over jeans to hide her porcine legs. Aaron dressed like Charles Starkweather, those days when he wandered student neighborhoods, a plain tee shirt tight over his weakling chest, blue jeans fitting loose on his skinny hips. He hoped his wispy mustache and brown felt hat made him look like the singer of a band.

Elisabeth was in the bathroom. Aaron talked to her from the adjacent room anyway, reciting the records in her collection that he approved of. *Pet Sounds* and *John Wesley Harding* and *Once Upon a Rhyme.* She laughed at him when she returned.

"You know I wasn't standing behind you anymore."

"Don't worry about it," he said.

It felt safe there, warm in a boozy way.

"Would you dance with me?" he asked, stepping into her space.

The LP he'd put on was a live recording of Piaf. It was warped and scratchy. Elisabeth blushed when it started playing. Surprised he'd picked her favorite.

# How to Die Young in a Nebraska Winter

I listened to sound of my parents dressing in the dark. It felt like I'd fallen asleep just a few minutes before, still night. I heard them in their closet through the wall. A jacket hanger pulled from the rack, the slide of plastic on oak, the pulling of a zipper. These were sounds I'd memorized, my father getting ready for work. He sighed as he sat on the bed. Mom helped with the suit jacket, letting his arms in before sliding it up and over his shoulders. She flattened the lapels and patted the shoulders and spoke some trembling magic into his ear.

I sat up on my elbow and hushed my brother's name across our room.

"Todd. Are you awake?"

"Be quiet. It's just Dad." Todd was two years older. He was about to turn thirteen and spoke in a soft, deepening voice. "Go to sleep," he said.

It was five in the morning when Charlie, our father, came to wake us. We sat on the beds, bare legs hanging down, crouched over to hold our water, feet pale and freezing in the early morning air. We were old enough to know something was wrong.

Mom came and stood between the beds in front of Charlie. She tried to explain things to us. Nothing came except a mournful vibrato. She couldn't say what had happened, so Charlie turned her around, pulled her into his chest, one hand steady in her curly, black hair, one hand smoothing out her tremors.

Charlie looked at us over her shoulder. He was getting old in a visible way. His cheeks were full, red and flaky after shaving. His ears hung big off the side of his head.

"Brandon asphyxiated last night." Charlie was a lawyer, he was good at breaking bad news. "Brandon was goofing around and choked on popcorn. The choking triggered an asthma attack. That's what killed him."

Services were held at a Presbyterian church in Bancroft that smelled like formaldehyde. All churches have smelled the same way to me since.

If Brandon had died in a bigger city we could have gone to a funeral home, but in places like Bancroft everything was done at the church. The visitation and the funeral and the reception after the burial. In a few days, on Sunday, normal services would resume. It was the same backdrop for weddings and baptisms too, red curtains and stained glass, polished organ pipes. There was a small room adjacent to the sanctuary that stored variations of plastic foliage for the ceremony that occasioned them. Its door was open when we arrived. We weren't supposed to see those blooms of celebration, the Christmas poinsettias, the Easter lilies. A woman closed the door, and I was relieved she did.

I stared at my feet the whole visitation. My shoes were black suede, stained a cloudy white by road salt. The laces were dirty gray. I wasn't prepared for this kind of thing to happen. My suit was stiff, bought the day before, and I refused to wear the new shoes that came with it. Todd and I sat in the second pew, hands between our knees.

Brandon's mother was a woman Charlie knew from college named Brenda. She had red hair and was muscular in a rural way. Apparently she and Charlie hooked up at a party the summer before his first year of law school, sitting in each other's arms next to a bonfire and drinking keg beer before moving to the backseat of his car. She was just visiting for the weekend and was back in Bancroft before the afterglow wore off. When Charlie found out she was pregnant he made it clear that he was willing to take responsibility for the kid, to finance the pregnancy and pay child support, or for an abortion if she wanted one. Marrying Brenda, however, was not an alternative. That wasn't the life he'd planned—Brenda wasn't the kind of woman he wanted as a wife. Her family was angry but there was nothing they could do about it. Charlie was hours away, and his parents supported his decision. "I feel horrible about it," he told her. "I'm going to pay for my mistake, but there's nothing else I can do."

She sat in front of us during the visitation, talking with my mom about Brandon while Charlie stood off to the side. Brenda and my mom didn't usually talk, but they drew solace from each other in that moment, the two moms. After the funeral, it would never be that civil again.

All ten rows of pews in the sanctuary were full. Most of the townsfolk knew who I was even though I'd never met them. They were the middle-aged friends of Brenda who'd seen us drive through their town with Brandon. They wore polo shirts and blue jeans and smelled like aftershave, like they were going to a country club dance. Some of them talked in the back but most kept silent. When anyone parted their lips to speak, most all the townspeople stared at them. They mostly watched Charlie. My father was the type of man who made enemies.

"How is everyone?" Pastor Harold sat next to Brenda in the front pew. "I hope we're all hanging in there."

"We're okay," Brenda told him. She handed out Kleenexes. "We're keeping it together."

"We're each other's backbones," my mom said.

"That's right," Pastor Harold agreed. "These are strong families. Families with roots that run deep and broad. This is never easy, but there's experience to draw on here." He motioned to Brenda's parents. "Together, you will all make it through this."

The reverend's mouth seemed to move automatically. I wondered if, after a while, being a clergyman was little more than breaking bread and drinking wine. An old man rubbing his hands together, turning dust to dust.

**B**randon's was the first funeral I went to. It amazed me how much sadness there was. Adults lost their composure. They huddled together to bawl on each other's shoulders. I wondered if all funerals were so hard. For me, it wasn't because Brandon was barely a teenager when he died—being young, I didn't grieve for lost youth—but because of how it made me feel to watch others grieve. And in the way outsiders treated me, offering condolences like I was part dead myself.

I didn't tell anyone this, but if it had been somehow necessary that Brandon die at that moment, then I wished that he'd killed himself. Then there would have been something to blame. Somehow this would have been an acceptable cause and effect. I'd heard of this happening, at least, learned about it on TV and in school. There would have been physical satisfaction in imagining this. The cool metal slipping between his lips. The buzzing sensation at the back of his cranium. Then the bloom. I could have understood that. It would have made sense to jump off a boat into the waiting mouth of a shark. Dying from asthma made no sense.

How Brandon died was obscene, but it fit the surroundings. I had to remind myself that it was late November in Nebraska. My half-brother hadn't wanted to die, after all. He hadn't planned any of this.

**B**randon was a regimented kid. He learned to paint by numbers. He'd just turned fifteen and wasn't unathletic when he could keep his breath. He was a strong reader of Gothic fiction and graphic novels. He woke up at 6:30 to eat three bowls of Lucky Charms every morning before washing his face. He knew a lot about American history, especially as it related to General Motors and Spider-Man.

We saw Brandon pretty often growing up. He was brought along for most of our family vacations. We picked him up from Bancroft for Thanksgiving and Christmas. Charlie stuck true to his promise, being responsible for his first son. They tossed around a football in the fall, saw a couple games at Wrigley in the summer if there were tickets. Brandon was buddies with our father in a way Todd and I never were.

Brenda must have been relieved that Charlie was never a stranger to Brandon. Her parents were supportive—they owned the hardware store in town—and her brothers and sisters helped out when they could, but it must have weighed heavily on her that she wasn't strong enough, or financially secure enough, to move away on her own. She dreamed aloud of her and Brandon starting over in a new place but was never able to follow through with those plans. She relied on her parents to keep going.

Brandon had been jaundiced and colicky as a baby, and in some ways he never grew out of it. With his asthma, whatever house they lived in was too moldy in summer and too drafty in winter. He couldn't always run with the other kids but was bright enough to hold his own. There were many things he was good at, non-sequiturs and puzzles.

He was an intelligent kid, there was no doubt. He'd had a lot of potential but was mostly an expert at becoming sick. If there was to be a manual for how to die young in a Nebraska winter, he could have written it.

**W**hen Charlie took me up to the casket, Brenda's boyfriend, Monte, was running his fingers through Brandon's hair. Brandon had thin blond hair and blue stitches in his scalp, with dried blood around the thread. His face was powdery and white. The makeup they put on Brandon made him look girlish.

Monte wore a white shirt. A tiger tattoo on his forearm showed beneath rolled-up sleeves. He asked my father about the stitches in Brandon's scalp.

"They have to do an autopsy," Charlie explained. "It's state law when a child dies. They need a sample of the brain."

Monte fingered the stitches. He touched the made-up face and cried under his breath, shaking his head.

"Little guy didn't deserve it," he said, trailing off. "Some stupid shit, this happening."

Charlie put his hand on Monte's back.

**W**hen Brandon stayed with us, while our new house was being built, he spent most of his time in the swimming pool. This was the summer before he died. To save money on condo rent, Charlie had his dream house put up in sections so we could live in the first half while the second was being finished. This is why Todd and me shared a bedroom that year.

Our house abutted a golf course. The swimming pool overlooked the seventh green. Brandon showed us how to time our cannonballs to mess up a golfer's putt. We floated in the pool on inflatable mattresses, sipped on Mountain Dew slushies, watched the construction crew work on the house, until Charlie came home from the law firm where he had just made partner.

Brandon was a serious kid—while we watched cartoons in the afternoon, he read Russian novels that I wouldn't pick up until college—but the pool helped him be immature. We had tea parties at the bottom, sinking plastic lawn furniture in the deep end then holding our breath while he poured imaginary Earl Grey and served raisin scones like my mom did for her friends. This was when *Jurassic Park* came out, so we pretended to be underwater raptors tearing each others' flesh. He taught us how to snorkel, to float on our bellies at the surface, telling us what to visualize when we looked at the bottom of the pool. Sometimes he imagined he was a microorganism wading in a petri dish. Or a man whacked by the mafia, adrift facedown in the harbor.

He stayed with us for three weeks that summer. Charlie made sure the pool was finished before Brandon arrived because he knew how much his first son liked to swim. There wasn't a public pool in Bancroft, so our vacations with Brandon always revolved around swimming or a body of water. Charlie liked to show Brandon things he normally couldn't see—things that one isn't able to experience in landlocked Nebraska.

We never used the pool much after the summer Brandon stayed in the new house. There were no swim parties for my birthday, no lazy days tanning beside the water. Mom quit cleaning it the next summer, so the water turned green, the blue-tile bottom slicked with algae. It would have been vulgar to swim in the pool then. After a few years Charlie quit calling the service to uncover and fill the pool in late spring. The tarp was replaced every fall, but there was never water underneath.

It's hard to think about what it meant to Charlie to keep the pool covered and dry. To see it each morning while he sipped coffee at the kitchen window, staring at the mesh tarp layered over with snow or leaves. When he and Mom had dinner parties, he was the one who explained why we didn't fill the pool. He never mentioned Brandon, but people seemed to know his death had something to do with it. It's too much hassle, Charlie would say. Too costly to repair the pump. Too dangerous for the boys. Eventually he said the damn thing leaked, glancing at the empty pool with anger in his eyes. People knew not to talk about it then.

The cemetery was at the top of a hill, on the outside of town where ponderosa pines coalesced along gravel roads and fields squared-in the acre where Brandon would be buried. There was an area for Protestants on one side of the highway and plots reserved for Catholics and Ponca Indians on the other. Brenda's parents had given one of their own plots for Brandon. When they died, they would share one, buried one on top of the other.

Charlie left the engine running during the interment so I could stay in the car. My nose ached. It had been running thin mucus all day, but was dry then. My nostrils felt wide open and my sinuses burned. My parents and Todd sat with their arms wrapped around each other under the funeral home tent, near Brandon's casket, Brenda and Monte next to them. A wispy snow fell. Small pellets were pressed to ice on the ground in the shape of footprints. I curled up in the backseat, too tired to watch.

I imagined what it would have been like to be there when Brandon died, plotting out the manual. Brandon dancing around the living room, lifting his knees above his waist, arms churning, a big goofy grin. He stops. Coughs out half-chewed bits of popcorn, hands at his throat, fingers probing his mouth. He looks at Brenda, eyes watering, then walks to her. She asks him what's the matter, pats his back then moves behind him for the Heimlich. This makes the boy vomit. They panic, recognizing an asthmatic fit, but he's still choking. It would happen too quickly to really know what was what.

Of course, I was grateful I wasn't there. I appreciated that I was allowed to use my imagination instead of having to remember actual details. Still, for many years, I had to watch it in parts, what I could imagine, with eyes closed at high school football games and in conversation at pancake feeds.

It wasn't until the families were at the burial that Brenda broke down, sitting there in the tent next to Charlie. After Pastor Harold blessed the body, as they prepared to lay Brandon at peace, Brenda leaned over and cried on Charlie's shoulder, softly, in the language of grief. She pulled his arm and mouthed the word *bastard*. Charlie said nothing in return. She stood to scream at him, spitting, tried to curse him to the ground. Monte held her from behind, pulled her back. She kept screaming.

Sitting up in the backseat to see the commotion, my vision blurry from tears, I heard Brenda's voice. I peeked over the door on my knees, my hands pressed to the glass. She stared at Charlie, standing above him, her face red and wet, her mouth open. She gasped for air with screams. Then her men surrounded her. Her father helped Monte pull her away.

Charlie hurried to the car. Mom's high heels slipped on the ice but Charlie caught her before she fell. He held the door and helped her into the passenger's side.

"It's okay," my mom told Charlie. "No one thinks it's your fault."

"The woman's crazy. She has every right to be crazy and she is."

"It isn't your fault," my mom insisted. "You're a great dad."

Charlie said he knew that. He put the car in drive then rode the brakes as he wove down the narrow brick roads of the cemetery hill, slowly, slowly, not an ounce of panic.

I asked my mom if we were going back to the church for the reception.

"Of course," she said. "People will get excited. But we have every right to be there."

**B**randon had been rushed to the emergency room because of asthma attacks before. There were trips for bronchitis and heat-seeking infections that had no reasonable cause.

Todd and I once joined our father to deliver a prescription to Bancroft that Brandon needed. It was late and the small-town pharmacies were closed, so we drove in from Lincoln, stopping in Omaha at the all-night Walgreen's before heading north on a two-lane highway. Charlie had made the trip a few times before that I'm able to recall.

It seemed like someone was playing a practical joke on us when we left that night. Charlie was so reserved. He drove below the speed limit. He stood with his hands in his pockets at the pharmacy counter as he hummed along with a song playing in his head. He paid with a credit card, which was an involved process in those days.

Brenda had a white two-story house with green trim across from the Methodist church in Bancroft. I recognized Monte's car slumped in the carport, his red Monte Carlo. Even then it was an unfunny joke that he drove that car. Branches from oak trees littered the damp, early spring grass. We climbed those trees with our mom when we came to visit Brandon because Mom didn't like being in Brenda's house. Mom was short and had strong legs that were perfect for climbing. She would swing herself onto a low branch and dart up to the middle of the tree, daring us to follow. She'd leverage and tilt herself up the tree until the limbs began to bend under her, cradled in a bough we were too chicken to reach.

We looked back at the street from the porch that night and watched a car turn the corner. Its headlights were off. Two men were in the car, but I couldn't see them distinctly. It was an older vehicle, something big, a Caprice. The men looked like gangsters to me, staring right at us as they were, but they were probably just farmers. Some guys drinking beers in their car that saw us drive by. People were protective of their own here. They noticed outsiders in expensive cars, like whatever year M5 Charlie drove then. He always drove a black BMW.

Charlie put his palm on Todd's shoulder, he grabbed my hand and pulled to the door. We went in without knocking.

Monte slipped around the corner to greet us when he heard the door and accepted the white paper bag with the prescription in it. He stood with Charlie and talked baseball, moaning over roster moves the Cubs had made, before taking the medication to Brandon. Monte was really fond of Charlie, even as a boy I recognized this. He looked up to my father and tried to appear interesting when he was around him, asking Charlie's opinion on sports and politics. Monte was a farmhand and did odd jobs around town in winter. He didn't have a trade, but he was usually good at helping.

In the other room I saw Brandon sit up on the couch, gagging on his breath with a pillow hugged between his knees. Brenda rubbed his back and attempted a smile for us.

"How are you boys?" she asked, her voice smoky. Curly red hair fell over her face.

Monte told us that there were video games in Brandon's room. Charlie nodded that it was okay, so we ran upstairs, treading the risers with both hands and feet like our greyhound climbed the stairs at home. The carpet was sticky and smelled like cigarettes.

In Brandon's room, a small television sat on the floor next to leather-bound volumes of adventure fiction. We left the lights off and turned the volume down. Grabbed Nintendo controllers and sat on Brandon's bed. We played *Tecmo Bowl* for a while, without passion, in the mechanical way kids pass time when their parents are busy. It was only the third quarter when Charlie yelled up the stairs that we needed to leave, and it didn't bother us that the game wasn't finished.

Brenda and Brandon were still on the parlor couch when we came down. He looked better then, sucking vapor from an inhaler. I thought his inhaler was bug repellent the first time I saw it, the blue plastic cartridge and white spray. We were at the park in Bancroft, whipping each other off the merry-go-round. Sitting in the gravel, I misted some on my legs. "Don't do that," Brandon said, pulling it away from me. "It's expensive."

**T**here was a great deal of talk about medications at the reception. Brenda had to be knocked out because she'd tumbled into a state of hysteria. There was speculation about what prescriptions would be forthcoming.

I didn't understand why a mother would have to be put under after her child died.

"It's common," my mom explained. We were on a walk in the park near the church. "There's a special bond between a mother and her child. Emotionally. Spiritually. It comes from being in the womb. A physical connection. A child should never die before their parent. It's too much to bear."

"I get that," I said. "But why the drugs? Why can't she be awake?"

"When I was a kid, the mother wouldn't even be at the funeral. She'd still be at home recovering. It's a great physical burden. The soul takes extra energy to keep going."

She smiled and pet the back of my head, frustrated by my incomprehension. It should have been intuitive to feel what she felt. To know what it's like from both ends.

"It's hard to explain," she admitted.

We walked with our coats open. It had stopped snowing, but the crooked sycamores in the park were frosted white. It felt good to walk like this with my mom. It reminded me of why I loved her. She was willing to tell me things that others weren't, to let me in on the secret tricks of becoming a person. She would reveal a lot about my father, when I was older, that I couldn't have known otherwise. All my knowledge, in one way or another, started with my mom.

"Is it a cheat?" I asked, tracing tree limbs with my eyes. "Just a little cheat, right? Because no one wants to see a kid die. It's too sad to see it through the mom's eyes. With that bond."

"Sure," my mom conceded. She sucked her lips. "You could put it that way."

She stopped on the sidewalk and braced my shoulders with her hands. She crouched down to my level.

"You should appreciate the bond most of all. Not the cheat."

Charlie never recovered. He never integrated back into our family because he couldn't feel comfortable. I could see this, even though it took me years to understand why. Charlie couldn't even sit or breathe without thinking of his lost son. I've come to understand this too. There isn't a graduation or wedding that goes by that I don't think of Brandon and his lost inheritance—these acts of comfortable living that somehow make my family complicit in his death.

My father spent time in the hospital a couple years after Brandon died. He hadn't been to the office in days. His body ached all over. He asked Mom to drive him to the hospital one night after dinner. We visited him every evening he was there and he was glad to see us. Mom reminded us to tell him he was a great dad as we walked in from the parking lot. He was excited that there was free pop on his floor, which was strange because we had cases of it at home. His face was like a child's, sneaking us treats from the galley. He said he missed us so much.

When he came home things were marginally better. He went to the office every day and was home for dinner, but he never again showed that childlike, desperate love for his family that he showed in the hospital. He was worn out and slept on the couch with the TV on when he wasn't at the office. He didn't like to talk, not to anyone. Mom had us make cards for him on his birthday, even though we were too old for that, trying whatever she could think of to make things better. We painted *Father of the Year* on the side of coffee mugs.

**B**etsy Updike ran across the parking lot when Aaron took her picture, hands up to cover her face. She was heavy and short and stomped when she ran. She wore horn-rimmed glasses. Aaron chased after to tell her he meant no harm. This was outside the Von Maur. It was a cold, breezy day.

"I love your hair," he said. "That's why I was shooting a photo of you."

Betsy wore a cardigan and had dark wavy hair that washed over her shoulders. She showed her teeth when she smiled.

When they got back to her house Aaron brushed her hair and they watched some movies she'd recorded on video tapes. He liked sitting behind her on the couch, his legs wrapped around hers, smelling the fruit of her shampoo. Betsy was a sweet girl. She was so eager to be loved that she nearly knocked Aaron over when they hugged.

# Impertinent, Triumphant

She looked beautiful, of course. She had a long neck and a small face, lovely gray eyes. That's why I kept looking. Her hair was wavy from some chemical treatment, and a dull, dull orange meant to be blond. She wore a terrycloth shirt, khaki shorts and leather sandals. She was really quite common. Modest chest, soft legs, a little bump where her stomach rose. I'd never seen a grown-up look so bored before, the way she slumped in her chair. I thought she was stunning.

There was a toy radio she listened to at her table, a tier below me on the hotel terrace, three patio umbrellas over. I noticed because the radio wasn't an iPod, but a yellow plastic toy with a drawstring that fit over her hand, with black rubber grips and built-in speakers so everyone had to listen to what she played, a political call-in show.

I couldn't turn away. Her face was round. The baby fat on her cheeks made her look younger than she was. She was nearly thirty, I'd learn. Her skin was firm and limpid as she sipped an Arnie Palmer with lips imperceptibly open.

We fought on the departing flight, my wife and I, on our way to Atlanta. She'd been hired to lecture about her work to the visual arts students of Emory. We always fought on airplanes, which made the fact that Jacq insisted I fly with her all the more maddening. Air travel set us off. We're not alone in this, of course.

We lived in Alliance, Nebraska, and had been packed into a commuter turboprop at the airfield, a plane so small I couldn't even sit up straight in my seat. I'm bigger and taller than a lot of people, but not so much that I don't usually fit in an airline seat. I had to sit with my neck crooked. It could be that this made me ready for confrontation. But it was Jacq who brought along that fashion rag and let it sit open on her lap. There was a spread about a designer she knew from New York, some Parisian who spent all his time with other people's spouses in Italy now. He insisted you call him Ampiere—his mother's maiden name—but his real name was Walt Watson. His father was Texan. Ampiere was a nuisance in our lives. I thought I'd buried the magazine in the recycling before Jacq saw it.

I wasn't going to say anything about the magazine that enraptured Jacq. I was going to hold my tongue and let her get this toxic energy out. So what if Ampiere was in a magazine. I was going to be a good husband, restrained, forgiving. I'd affect a touch of whimsy in the way I let my wife go on about an old flame. It only lasted until we were in the air. I couldn't stomach disrespect then.

"Just look at Ampiere." Jacq had to shout over the noise of the turboprop. "He always looks good on film, doesn't he?"

"Have you heard from him lately?" I asked. "Do you think he remembers you?"

"Him coming out of a pool isn't so bad either."

I don't recall much of what I said to her after that, but I remember every word of what she said to me. "Your job is the problem. A man shouldn't be home all the time. No one should be."

"After everything, and you still bring that up?"

"Oh, Sam. You're a decent man. Don't ruin yourself by trying to be clever."

It was painfully annoying, but such is any relationship. I didn't think it was a big deal. There was shouting, Jacq's purse was spilled. A flight attendant had to intervene, some exasperated bitch who stood over us and glared. Drink service was cancelled.

**I** spent the first evening on the hotel terrace waiting for Jacq to return from Emory. My clothes were drenched with sweat —it was summer in Atlanta, in 2009—and I was thirsty for bourbon and fruit. Jacq was out with the department chair, some art students tagging along, maybe an assistant dean. It wouldn't be late when she returned to the hotel, shortly after midnight. She'd be pumped up, though, on booze and admiration. She felt her success most tangibly when around sycophants. I felt it too.

My wife could be unbearable when she was pleased with herself—I think she knew this—so it was unfortunate she was such an accomplished woman. She was an artist—wiry strong, lean, all bones and muscle—and very busy. The fees she collected for lectures and appearances provided for our lifestyle, but that also meant she was expected at parties and openings most of the year, in far-flung conference rooms and auditoriums. Her profession demanded she travel. I travelled with her. She needed me to keep her grounded, to talk back. That's why I had to go with her on airplanes; that, and because she feared we'd die apart. She couldn't stomach the idea of dying without me.

Jacq was supposed to visit a gallery in Savannah the next day where a collector had bought one of her collages. This was a seminal piece for her, one she hadn't seen for years, and she was eager to reconnect with it. Jacq's meme consisted of landscape art she made with tufts of prairie grass and matted buffalo hair. She had a peculiar relationship with her patrons, I thought, because of her medium. Most people knew her from her early work, when she reconstructed the sediment record of canyons with menstrual blood and acrylics. The pieces were really quite accurate, in a way. She often overstated line and could have made bolder use of color and space, but it didn't really matter what I thought. I did product descriptions for a conglomerate of online specialty stores. It was all niche stuff—we rode the coattails of SkyMall—nothing I'd buy myself. The job was done mostly through e-mail and that meant I could travel freely. I didn't need to work, but I liked having something to do. There's joy in being recognized as good at something, no matter how insignificant that thing is.

Maybe that's why I couldn't stand being around people who adored Jacq's work. I didn't exist to her admirers. Actually, it was worse than that. They saw me, they knew I was Jacq's husband, and just wished I wasn't there. At galleries, museums, private showings, art schools, universities—it was all the same. Whether they were trendy or rustic, retro or futuristic, queer or confused, they all made vile faces at me, using the tannins of a bitter wine to twist their mouths. They're sinister people.

I assumed Jacq messed around. She's an artist, after all, and it was easy to believe in the trappings of that identity. Beautiful, stylish people could be persuasive, young men whose pants bulged, experienced women who did interesting things with their smiles and stroked Jacq's jaw with their long fingers. She might have had flings, spontaneous encounters, maybe in a gallery restroom while I was occupied at a crowded opening night soirée. It was possible such things happened. Most people would understand how that worked. Jacq had a history, a notorious past her friends liked to reminisce about, a young woman in the city. You can do the math.

When we met, Jacq said she liked me because I was stable. "A nice, trustworthy man," she called me. It sounded like an insult coming from her.

Sitting out on the hotel terrace in Atlanta that first night, ruminating over a neat bourbon, I thought that an affair of my own was a distinct possibility. If Jacq had done it, so could I. I watched the girl with the toy radio stare off into the distance, listening to talk; I worried about what Jacq might do with the assistant dean, or a visiting professor from Lyons, if there was one. There's something noble, isn't there, about being the second one in a marriage to stray. If you are the aggrieved and you stand up for yourself, people should applaud.

Jacq went to Savannah the next day in a hired car. Riding in cars she managed fine without me. She liked talking to the driver, finding out about his family and where he came from. It's different with pilots, who you're not allowed to see work. With a driver, you know if they're paying attention, or if they've had a few drinks, or if they're sleepy. If they're sleepy, you can chat to keep them awake. Drivers like to chat. They never seem to be from the place where they are, so you can ask how they ended up in Georgia, driving Lincoln Town Cars. That's what Jacq would do. She grew up in Ohio, the third daughter of auto workers, and ended up spending most of her life in New York City, painting with her menstruations. She understood better than most how funny life could be.

I saw the girl on the hotel terrace again that evening. She was at the same table as before. When I asked about her, the waiter told me she'd been there all day. "All week, sir, to be exact. Hasn't moved as far as I seen. She just sit with that radio."

She was pale, which was odd for a young woman in that climate. She sat near the rail, dabbling at ranch dressing with raw vegetables, drinking some sour cocktail through a straw. A wispy linen dress hung from her shoulders. She held the toy radio, the drawstring loose around her wrist. I asked if there was any way I could help.

"I'm sorry," she said. "With what?"

"You seem stifled. Are you all right?"

"Me?"

"That radio, for example. It's such a strange thing. Something a kid would carry."

"This? It's nothing," she said. "Just the news. I like to hear the weather. Though they're arguing over the school board now."

"Do you mind?" I asked, scraping over a cast-iron chair to join her.

She extended her hand. "I'm Anna," she said. She turned off the radio and dropped it into her purse.

Anna told me she was visiting from St. Louis while her house was under reconstruction. Her husband suggested, and she consented, that it would be more enjoyable for her to take a vacation than wait until the house was no longer a disaster area. He would summon her when the work was done.

She asked if I was married and I didn't lie—I was an apparent tourist, middle-aged, in khaki shorts, wearing my wedding band. I had a walker's physique: fit in some places, not so much in others. I told Anna that my wife was an artist. Anna's husband worked in government, she said. He wanted to be elected to high office some day. He worked campaigns for principals in the local party now, as many as he could get in on. In fact, that's how she met him. She'd been an intern for Kit Bond while an undergrad at SLU.

"Wish I could do more for him," she said, "career-wise. Besides making a family, I mean. We don't have babies," she added, quietly.

When Anna talked about how practically everyone who mattered in St. Louis knew who her husband was and what he wanted, it sounded like she despised him for his ambition. She had a habit of glaring at her hands when she spoke. She confessed that she had no idea what she was doing in Atlanta.

"My neighbor set up the trip, honestly. Rita came over and used our computer to do it. What did she call this place? *Hotlanta*?" Anna grinned as she said this, hand over her mouth. "She said something about the heat and how it made folks hunger. My neighbor is a lonely woman, I think. I don't know why I trust her."

Anna picked at celery stalks as she talked. She somehow managed to not take bites when she put food to her mouth—she bit without biting through—there were teeth marks in the carrots on her plate. She'd only ordered because the waiter kept asking if she wanted something.

We talked about marriage a long time. The good stuff, then the bad, then the qualifications and excuses. Our conversation followed a plot arc. Something happened to Anna, she was emotional, she calmed down, something else happened a few weeks after that, and it wasn't until later that she remembered the first thing, the original outrage, and by then it was too late for her to do something about it. Her resentment piled up. My stories were the same, structurally. We turned listless and bleak, hearing about each other's marriage wounds. They lacked finality. We wanted firm endings and closure.

Neither of us had been to Atlanta before. We talked about being there. It was something different to talk about, something universal to our kind, being on vacation.

"I haven't even left the hotel yet," Anna confessed. "I took a taxi cab from the airport. I've been here ever since."

I convinced her that we should see some sights together. Jacq would be in Savannah all the next day too.

"We should go to the MLK stuff, at least. I need someone to see it with. You can't go to things like that alone. People will think you're up to something."

Jacq almost married Ampiere, years ago, a few months before she met me. He backed out before they had anything legalized. They'd been together for years, off and on. Jacq adored him. She followed him around and let him introduce her to people. There were blurbs about them in the *Village Voice*, the *Post*, elsewhere. Ampiere was prone to grand, meaningless gestures, the kind of sadism women found charming. Jacq let Ampiere have his way with her. He didn't want to marry her, however. He made this clear, in a hotel room with a half-dozen aspiring male models, then fled to Europe after 9/11 because he was too anxious to stay. To her credit, Jacq didn't chase him there. She couldn't hold it against him, I don't think, his betrayal. She didn't have it in her to hate Ampiere. If he wanted to fly off to Italy to explore bodies she would let him. Jacq was fine with staying in New York. She had her own occupation, after all.

Even if she let Ampiere go, I don't think she ever really got over him. That's why the magazine bugged me so much on the way to Atlanta. There he was, in swimming briefs and black sunglasses, with a woman who was too beautiful for him.

Jacq once went into detail about their sex life, after I dared her to. We were on a hotel balcony in Los Angeles, the night after she met design students at Otis. It was late and we'd drunk enough to say stupid things. "He's hard all the time, you know. It never goes away. He fucked me till I bled. He came on my tits. I'd be soaked all over, in both his and mine. We fucked in half the public washrooms of New York, I'm sure." How could I forget these things? "He had me go down on him in theaters, in changing rooms; I took his fingers in cabs, on the subway. In restaurant washrooms he entered from behind and came inside me. Old Ampiere. There's a man with guts."

She would deny these things were true, later, like such denials could mean something. They meant nothing. We'd never live down that monologue, I didn't think. Even if the marriage ended, the declaration she made that night, that anthem she sang bitterly and clear, would live on.

**A**nna wanted to take a cab to Auburn Avenue, but I convinced her to ride the train with me. We went to Underground Atlanta first to shop for souvenirs. Anna bought a Braves hat for her husband. "I'm sure he won't wear it," she said. "He only wears Cards hats and Pujols jerseys. It's politics." She bought a tube of M&Ms for no real reason. They were there. After that we bought Coke floats from a vendor and sat on a rubbery green bench to fish globs of soft serve from cups. Anna took the toy radio from her purse and set it between us on the bench. "Just so we don't get bored," she said.

I told a story from my childhood about how I picked up walnuts from the lawn before my dad mowed. (I don't know what brought this up. This was peanut country. Why should I think of Connecticut walnuts?) The shells dulled the blades if they were mowed over, so it was my job to collect them in a grocery sack and throw them away. We had a few walnut trees, all mature and thriving. Every summer we'd end up with hundreds of pounds of nuts. They were thick with green rind when they fell, nearly as big as baseballs sometimes, and they leaked a disgusting-smelling black juice that stained my skin. The juice would kill the grass if left to its purpose.

"I hated it so much," I told Anna. A voice cackled some grievance from the radio, suddenly loud. "But that was my job, every Saturday. Dad supervised from the patio. He'd notice if I missed any, then have me crisscross the lawn with a point of his finger."

Anna was very affected by the story. She grimaced. Her face glowed with sweat. "I did that for my dad too," she said, remembering. "And I still won't eat a walnut unless somebody makes me."

I was comfortable with women like Anna. I knew what to say to them and how I was expected to behave. I could listen without interrupting. These were things I learned in my old career, when I was a travel agent. I knew what kinds of courtesy pleased bourgeois women.

We visited Ebenezer Baptist after another train ride. At the back of the pews we stood close and stared ahead, watching tourists photograph each other. I felt guilty being there. The church didn't mean much to me. It was famous. I'd seen it in movies, on the History Channel. There wasn't any reason for me to be there, except to be there with Anna. It was different for other people. There were big families alive with sweat and laughter, some in tears. This was a pilgrimage to them. They dressed in colorful, stiff dresses, in purple silk shirts and black slacks. There was an old man with a white mustache who wore a suit and hat. He leaned on a three-pronged aluminum cane. These people hugged and took photos, ones they would show off to folks back home, I imagined.

At the Martin Luther King tomb, Anna and I sat by each other on the edge of the fountain that surrounds it, sharing a bottle of soda in the sun. Anna sat with her legs crossed, a pleated skirt floating on her thighs. We stared into the mirrored glass across from us and listened to the rippling water. I recognized a few people from Ebenezer who were doing the same self-guided we were, the old man with the cane. Anna talked about her husband again. She was supposed to call him during the day, after lunch, and in the evening after dinner. But she didn't that day. She wondered if he missed her call, or if he was too busy to notice.

Anna talked about her husband a lot. What food he ate, what clothes he wore, what movies he didn't care for. She talked about his parents and friends, his sleeping habits. I felt oddly close to Anna when she talked about Jon—and to him too. I didn't know this man, I'd never met or heard of him, but I was privy to his private details. She told me his shirt size, where he went to high school, the names of his siblings, what he smelled like after wearing a suit all day in the hot summer sun. I wondered if Anna had a pet name for his penis, and if she did, what that pet name was. Did she call it Napoleon, his dick? Mama's little helper? The long, lazy weekend? The fund-raiser? I don't know why, but every detail she told about him seemed to offer some clue as to what she might have called his prick. I fed all the information she shared into the game, hand on my chin, deep in thought, as if this was a code I could eventually crack.

I didn't actually like hearing about him, the game aside. At the tomb I couldn't help myself. I said, "You talk about him too much."

"Who? Jon?"

"Yes."

"I'm sorry."

"You don't have to be sorry. It's fine for a woman to talk about her husband." I put a hand on her back and apologized for saying anything. I'd merely wanted to interrupt her, I think. "I don't care to hear about men I've never met. That's all."

She fumbled to adjust her sunglasses, turned the toy radio off. She was shaking.

"What will we do tonight?" I asked. "I'd like to drive somewhere, if we had a car."

Anna let her eyes flicker behind her sunglasses. She didn't have anything else to say. I looked at her eyes through the dark lenses, and, holding her arms at her sides, I kissed her. Her mouth opened, although she didn't press back. I tasted the sugar on her lips, from the Coke, and breathed in the chlorine mist of the fountain.

We looked around as if we expected to be caught when the kiss was over. We looked for anyone who might have seen. It was just the old black man with the mustache who looked, hat tilted back on his skull, leaning on that three-pronged cane.

Jacq returned from Savannah the next afternoon. She wanted to tell me about her time with the collector, but I wouldn't listen. I told her I'd be staying in Atlanta. She would not be. I told her there was a return ticket booked in her name. She'd fly back to Alliance without me. Jacq didn't care for the idea. She threw a fit in the cab, and I had to check her bag for her. It wasn't until she was in line at security that she finally relented. Jacq couldn't resist a parting shot, not in an airport. She said she was happy to be rid of me for a few days. "Even if the plane crashes and I die," she said, "I'll be glad to do it alone."

**I** knew Anna would be waiting on the terrace the next morning. She knew I'd come sit with her. We lounged in the patio chairs and killed time and ate hungrily from a plate of melon and avocado slices. The air was heavy with smog and vapor, the sun already high. Plants had shot up all over the place, broad-leafed and waxy. Trees of heaven at the edges of parking lots, along the roadside, on the tops of hills. You couldn't stop them, it seemed. They grew too fast to get rid of. They sprouted everywhere.

Anna played her radio that morning. We talked some, but didn't have all that much to say. We'd seen each other again the night before for a movie at a mall theater near the hotel. There were drinks after that. We stayed up late talking. I didn't mention that Jacq went home. Anna didn't ask about my wife anymore, she didn't question where Jacq was. Anna was uncomfortable thinking about it. It was easier to talk about her husband, to talk about Jon, since she couldn't stop. I didn't mind talking about him then, not at breakfast anyway, since there were open spaces to stare off into, a busy thoroughfare nearby to watch cars. I'd listen enough to respond now and then, although it wasn't necessary. Anna just wanted to work her mouth.

I was thinking about pet names for pricks when I saw a Pomeranian wander out into the thoroughfare. I laughed when I saw it come out of the trees, a bouncing white puff of fur.

There was a neighborhood across the road, behind a trees of heaven clutch. The Pomeranian must have escaped from its yard and found its way to the thoroughfare, drawn by the noise. It looked pleased with itself as it approached the road, the way dogs do when they think they're getting away with something, when they're doing something stupid.

A woman gasped when she saw the dog, then everyone turned to the road, the traffic. Anna spun in time to see the Pomeranian struck by a car. We all saw. We all heard. The dog caught in the undercarriage of a gray Cadillac and spit out the back to tumble along the pavement. The Cadillac didn't stop. The cars behind slowed and bowed around the dog once they saw it heaped in the center lane. Anna wondered why no one stopped to help. She asked how the driver could do that.

"Maybe they didn't notice," I said. She didn't buy that.

"How couldn't they?"

Some hotel workers went out and circled the dog. They helped direct traffic and gave the appearance that things were under control. No one wanted to touch the dog. They surrounded it and talked. We couldn't hear what they said. "They're deciding who will pick it up," I guessed.

Eventually a man in a burgundy-red uniform came out and wrapped the dog in a pillowcase. He lifted it off the road and carried it to the parking garage.

**We** stayed in Anna's room after that. She turned on the TV. I took my shoes and socks off.

It was three days like that. Anna curled under the hotel comforter to watch basic cable, the air conditioning on full blast, while I typed on my laptop at the Lucite bureau. I had to catch up on work, but I crawled in next to her when I was bored and hugged her from behind. She wore pajamas, black and furry, that zipped up in the front. Anna and I never slept together. I enjoyed her body like I did comfort food, like too much might make me sick. We napped and dozed. I laid my hand on her tummy and felt how soft it was. I rested my head on her shoulder and smelled her hair. Sometimes she reared into me to spoon, but that was as far as it went.

We hardly even talked. Anna didn't mention Jon, not after what happened with the Pomeranian. She asked questions like we'd just met—which, I realized, was precisely the case.

"What's it like there, where you live?" Anna asked. "Are there any people in Nebraska? I couldn't live like that, out in the middle of nowhere. I get the creeps just thinking of all those cows out there, chewing grass."

Jacq and I had been married seven years by then. We met in New York and were married there. She's nine years older than me, from northwest Ohio originally. I grew up in Connecticut, in a banal, middle-class neighborhood, but the tiny travel agency I operated was in Chelsea. That's where I lived when we met. My parents started the agency in the seventies and it wasn't a bad business. We were a small outfit with regular clients. Then 9/11 happened. Almost all small agencies went out of business the next couple years. We were no different. My parents started the agency; it was shuttered on my watch. Then I started writing product descriptions for the online novelty mall. Then I married Jacq.

Once we were married Jacq convinced me to move out to the ranch she'd bought near Alliance. I had nothing else going. The agency was closed. My job with the Internet people was flexible. I felt like I might be getting a little old for New York. The idea of settling on the Ponderosa to grow into middle age sounded romantic. So we moved.

I liked it right away. There was a new house on the ranch —the hunting lodge, I called it—a guest house Jacq turned into her studio, plus lots of open valleys of dirt and rock I hiked in. I bought a pistol and a holster because there were coyotes, and damn if that didn't excite me. Alliance had a country club where we'd go for drinks sometimes if we wanted to trade stories with locals, and a RadioShack and a pharmacy and a pizza place. Most of our food was shipped to us from an organic market run by a disembodied poet in Boulder, but we frequented the greasy cafes and steakhouses if we felt tolerant of shredded iceberg lettuce and Folgers crystals. There was a swimming pool, a track at the high school. There was more than that, but those were the places we went to. The nearest Wal-Mart was in Scottsbluff, an hour away, so a few of the local stores in Alliance avoided being run out of business. I appreciated that.

There was lots of time on the ranch. I learned how to use it. I answered e-mails, worked on my descriptions. I began expansive, free-form landscape projects I never intended to finish, left mounds of worm castings and hardwood mulch to scatter across the prairie. I talked to my parents an hour every Sunday evening, something we did ever since I took over the agency from them. We didn't really know what to say anymore. Mostly they bitched about the commercials for Priceline and Travelocity they saw on TV. If I was bored, I trawled airfares on my computer, in the old system, a black screen with green characters. It was all prompt commands, no windows, no clicking a mouse. I loved it. It was like traveling back to a time when you had to be an expert to run a computer, the good old days.

It wasn't something I saw coming, but I liked living in a small town. (This is what I explained to Anna when she asked how I could stand a place like Alliance.) There's something essentially decent about walking on Main Street with the rumble of pickup trucks circling to cruise a highway drag, or happening into a park when the Legion team is on the diamond. You can stand at the fence and watch the game. "We love that," I said, sitting up out of Anna's blankets. "The little kids race into the weeds after foul balls. The fathers chain-smoke and lean into the backstop to grumble. At night you can see the dome of light from the highway."

**A**nna and I went out to a club in Buckhead, near the hotel. I'd been in Atlanta nearly a week. Anna wanted to go dancing, but the place we went to wasn't a real club. This was a suburban bar, across from the mall. There were TVs showing Braves highlights and old replays of Herschel Walker in a Sugar Bowl, years and years ago. The place made me feel my age. I was eight years older than Anna. That seemed like a big difference there. In reality, Anna was too old for this place too. It was all college students, or kids of that age, like a frat party. It made me nervous to see groups of young, drunk-fuelled men in college football tee shirts and jean shorts roaming the floor. I felt like such a Yankee. Most of my clothes were out with a laundry service, so I was in a black suit and white dress shirt I'd brought along just in case. I didn't wear the tie, but it still felt ridiculous to be dressed like this in a place like that. I wouldn't dance with Anna.

There was a group of guys at a table near us, Yellow Jacket fans, according to their branding. They flirted with Anna when they came for drinks at the rail, two or three of them at a time, asking her to dance. She was nervous about it. Her back straightened when they spoke to her. "No thank you," she said. "Not interested." I could tell she liked the attention. She refused them each time, even though she'd come here to dance.

"Why don't you tell them you're married," I said. "Say you're pregnant. Maybe they'll give up and leave you alone."

I saw by Anna's face that she liked those boys talking to her. The ones she'd already said no to watched out of the corners of their eyes, alert to what Anna would do next. She looked different, watching them back. By the angle her face tilted, how she swept her hair behind her ears, I saw how she betrayed different emotions. She didn't look so bored.

She asked one of them to dance with her, this after an hour of racing drinks. There wasn't really a dance floor, but they piped in a club mix and there was an open area Anna pulled the kid to. He had on a rugby shirt, striped blue and white. His hair was wet, his cheeks red, like he'd just been in the shower. Anna was obliterated, her limbs heavy with alcohol. She stumbled through raunchy, improvised steps. She wore a knee-length black cotton skirt the kid inched up her thighs. Her legs flexed and rattled, tendons showed behind her knees. She wasn't such a good-looking woman, that's why those boys liked her.

Jacq and I met at an opening, seven years earlier, in New York. I was barely hanging on to the agency then, it was 2002. I introduced myself at the wine table. It would have been more awkward to not talk, so we talked. Neither of us were native New Yorkers, but we'd both lived in the city a long time. It was so soon after 9/11. We were over-emotional, over-endangered, out to prove both our cowardice and bravery. It was silly. I'd never talked so much about pizzerias and bridges in my life—and prattled on about them with such strong affection, as if they were beloved grandparents or something.

We were such opposites on the surface. Jacq was tall and pale, with jaw-length black hair, so skinny that her chin and shoulders looked like parts of a performance piece. Her parents were auto workers. She was a painter…a mixed-media…a whatever—she didn't like having to explain to anyone what she did on canvas. She was (and still is) Jacqueline Ranier Roenicke; I was (and still am) Eric Samuel Green. I wore a tight brown cardigan, a shirt and tie underneath, wool-lycra trousers. I was a small-business owner, blond and pudgy. We were reverse parts of the same silhouette, and that's powerful magic. She turned me on the same way an accused witch would have aroused a priest in Salem, Mass., in 1692.

We ended up at a downtown bar. It was full of suits, market and city government dweebs who tried to act tough. They couldn't beat Jacq's testosterone, however. She tore up to the bar and ordered Tullamore Dew, neat. She told off anyone who got near us. She accused them of trying to sneak an inch in on her man. You could get most of those guys to turn red just by accusing them of the slightest hint of homosexuality. It was too easy.

She pulled me into the men's room near the end of the night. That's when she fell in love with me, or so the story goes. She fell in love because I wouldn't fuck her. I said we'd have to eat a meal first, at a table, with silver. She'd have to take me home before I'd make love with her. She kissed with her teeth while she laughed.

"Of course," she said. "How adorable!"

I laid it on a bit thick, of course. I wanted to fuck her badly. The problem was that I'd never been able to become rigid in a bathroom. I couldn't stomach the idea of those suit jocks listening to her moan, or them watching my ass dimple through the gaps of a stall divider. Bedrooms are made for sex. Wide mattresses, soft sheets, a ceiling fan rocking. This was the only audience I desired.

The wet-haired boy's frat brothers egged him on. They wanted Anna to pull her shirt up. They wanted her to go down on him in the storage room while all of them watched. She was in a lawless realm, boys rubbing the crotches of their jean shorts as they encircled her. One of them tugged her arm toward the back.

Anna looked to me, her face wrinkled in frustration, but I didn't move to help her. I leaned against the bar, nursing a bourbon and soda. When the song was over, she shook off the frat boys and slumped into the rail next to me. The kid she danced with asked her to come to a party with them. She told him to fuck off. We left soon after.

Anna collapsed in the hotel elevator. She said she was going to be sick. I had to carry her to her room, her words coming out backwards. I was sure security would follow us, but we made it through the door. She flopped to the couch.

When I jabbed Anna in the shoulder, her eyes rolled back in her head. Her bangs flipped around.

"What's wrong with you?" I said. "It's just some booze, you'll be all right."

We camped by the toilet most of the night. She slept on the tile with her knees at her chest, hands between her legs. "Take it easy," I said, curled around her body. My hand was on her stomach, my ear at her mouth to make sure she was breathing.

Her head cleared after a few hours. It was four in the morning and I hadn't slept. We were still on the floor of her bathroom. Anna shivered on the icy tile despite the comforter I wrapped around her. She was feeling better though, not so drunk anymore.

"What happened?"

"Nothing," I said. "You didn't do anything." I paused, looking at her until she shrunk away. "It wasn't anything unretractable," I said. "Just regrettable."

Anna buried her head in her hands to whimper.

She moved across the tile to where I sat against the bathtub. She nuzzled against my chest and pulled the comforter around us.

"What would I do without you?" she said. "You're a very brave man."

I didn't know what to say to that. I said nothing.

She continued on like that. I knew she was humoring me, trying to smooth things over. That's what I thought, anyway. Maybe she believed that I'd stepped in on her behalf, once those boys started to paw her, and swept her safely away. I hadn't.

"Sam," she said. "Tell me something nice."

Anna disappeared under the comforter. I felt her face through the fabric of my suit pants, the trembling vibrations of her breath. I didn't think to stop her. She unbuckled and unbuttoned and unzipped.

"Anna," I warned. "It's not going to happen in here."

But there it was. The thing popped up on its own—impertinent, triumphant—swaying out through my open zipper.

She put her mouth around the thing, her whole mouth, which somehow wasn't dry. It was melting. My hips lifted and arched as far as she allowed.

I stopped her then, while I still could.

"What are you doing?" I asked. Anna snuck out from the comforter to rest her head on my stomach and look up at me. "It's what I do," she said. "You know, to make amends."

She was not embarrassed to say this.

"That's what you do with Jon?"

She nodded.

"God," I said. "Just finish."

Jacq was waiting at the airfield outside Alliance the next evening. She was in the gravel parking lot, lying on the hood of the old truck she drove, an F-250 that came with the ranch when she bought it. She adopted that truck like an orphaned child. It suited her.

We bounced onto the bench seat and swung out on the highway to reach full speed, the windows down all the way, seatbelts flapping loud in the gale, tires gripping over the patched pavement. We smiled out over the land. Jacq looked different in Alliance, on our ranch, than she did in any city. She wore jeans and a loose flannel shirt with nothing underneath. I preferred her this way. She rolled her sleeves up. There was paint on her knuckles and dirt under her nails. She tied pigtails so that the rubber band ties snuck out under her straw hat. I saw inside her shirt as she drove, her small breasts swaying, bouncing with the rhythm the road gave them. Her chest pocked with moles, tanned deep and reddish in the big, rusty, Western sunset.

Lorna Chaplin flashed her cleavage over the orange Formica counter when she rang up his total. Aaron was buying a microwavable Rueben and a Diet Pepsi. She worked at a filling station near the interstate in Ralston and had dark freckles around her neck. She wore low-rise stonewashed jeans without a belt. When Aaron looked at her midriff he noticed a pink scar across her navel. She said, "My eyes are up here, honey."

He came back the next night to ask her out to the burger and gyro place down the road.

She lived in a small white house not far from the filling station. It had been her parents' house, the place she grew up in. All the old furnishings were still there, worn sofas, porcelain knickknacks on the wall. There were small wooden cups Lorna's father made in his basement workshop when he was alive. Lorna's eyes pinched nearly closed when she smiled. It was a nice smile, one that made Aaron think she'd been very pretty in high school.

Aaron liked talking to Lorna about her life. She got nostalgic and teary, muttered "son of a bitch" through dry nicotine lips.

She told him how most of her life was documented in the public record, in court cases and various judgments levied against her, in smarmy newspaper articles. There was a string of charges that ended with a conviction for transporting a minor across state lines—a fifteen-year-old boy listed in the record as N.S. And that's what she called the boy too, when she told Aaron about him, even though N.S. would be close to thirty by then, a man off living somewhere, with a family to take care of, more than likely. "I was pregnant by him when they picked us up," Lorna admitted. "But I don't have children of my own."

# Violate the Leaves

## 1

I found my mom fidgeting with her uniform in front of the bedroom mirror. The sand-dappled camo tee shirt that bit her armpits it was so tight. The black mascara, the no lipstick. Her hair coiled in a bun to fit under the squarish khaki hat. Her rucksack tied up tight and made to balance next to the closet door. It was early. She noticed me standing in the doorway and kept dressing. She stared into her eyes in the mirror and must have wondered what we were all wondering about, what the next year would bring. She sat to pull her boots on and started with the laces. "Go eat breakfast," she told me, "if you have to be up so early."

Downstairs my father was frying eggs. "What's the deal, Oscar?" he asked. I shook my head, turned away from him. I worried the waistband of my pajamas above my bellybutton. He picked me up and sat me on the counter. "It's just us now," he said. "Are we going to be okay?"

Later, I put on my brown suit, the new one from Sears. I'd thrown a fit in the store when my father suggested that some slacks with suspenders would be good enough for the party. I didn't want slacks with suspenders. I wanted to be as perfect as my mom was. I wanted to look neat and sleek and formal. I wanted a uniform.

## 2

The relatives drove in from different places. They'd left early in the morning, some of them the afternoon before, and were made lazy by their travels. They leaned on porch railings and sat sighing on the front steps. The smell of them as they lined up for photographs with my mom under the big oak tree in the yard. The Chicago cousins, all girls, announced themselves with sugary perfumes, like a magazine in the mailbox, and the flurry of teasing that burst out in their cutting city manners. Their hair was done up in curls if older, brushed down straight if nearer my age. And the billows of cigarette smoke, the hiked-up Wranglers of my uncles who stood away from the commotion to mumble gossip. I was eight years old and couldn't really talk to any of these men. They were what remained of my father's family, all of them bachelors or divorced, journeymen machinery workers in Des Moines. They poked boot tips at the roots of milkweed and tried to remember where the barn used to be, the gate to the hogs, the chicken hutch, the corrugated steel quonset where machinery had been held when this was still a family farm, the farm they grew up on, before all but what the house sat on was sold. They pointed to the oak tree where my Chicago cousins played on their cell phones, and debated about which ancestor it was who planted that tree, a red oak, no, a white oak, back when this land was settled.

There was vanilla ice cream with fresh strawberries after the bratwurst and burgers. There were sopapillas.

Grandpa Amos brought me a goldfish in a bowl. The fish was orange but shined when it spun in its water. After lunch I took the fish to my bedroom and refused to come downstairs.

"Come see your mother," Grandpa Amos said. He pounded a hand against the stairwell to make the walls thunder. There was no chance I'd come down after that.

I tried to get the goldfish to look at me but it wouldn't. It swam to the bottom and sucked on the green rocks there. Confused and overhot from the car ride. In the back of the bowl I saw my reflection. A blurrier, darker version of myself. Black circles under my eyes.

I wondered where Grandpa Amos bought the goldfish. It was a long drive from Cleveland to where we lived. We lived somewhat close to Des Moines. There would have been plenty of pet shops along the way.

The fish came from Indiana, I decided.

## 3

**I** stayed in my bedroom when it was time for her to leave. I didn't want to cry in front of my cousins from Chicago. I didn't want to cry in front of my mom.

## 4

I'd helped her pack that week. There were charms I stuck in her rucksack, thinking she wouldn't notice how I sneaked them there. The plastic cowboy that was my best toy. The poem about Santa dying in a sleigh wreck that I wrote for her during the second-grade holiday activities program, on green construction paper shaped like an evergreen tree. When she wasn't looking I wormed my Saint Christopher medallion deep into the rucksack, under her army clothes, under the magazines and manuals, to keep her safe when she was over there.

From outside the house I heard her calling. "Come to the window, mijo! I want to see you!"

The whole family waited under the oak tree. She was in her fatigues, less neat now, hair in her face, her face red. She was in the middle of the cousins from Chicago, who twisted their feet in the dusty yard.

"Come! This is the last time I'm telling you!"

My father stood by the car. I wanted it to be him who was leaving.

## 5

I lay on the bed listening to the curtains flap. The fishbowl sat on the desk. The fish circled in the fishbowl.

## 6

My father had a crippled arm. It was crippled in a car wreck the summer after he graduated high school. A friend of his rammed an SS Camaro through a construction barricade at eighty mph then continued at a slightly slower speed into the blade of a bulldozer. Nobody died. They were blotto drunk and that saved them. All were pulled bendable from the wreckage once the authorities arrived, lacerated and vomiting, but nearly pristine; still surly, the story goes, cussing out the cops for hassling them. My father's arm was the only casualty —made useless when the Camaro's motor was birthed through the firewall and pinned that side of him against the passenger door.

When I came downstairs—after the cousins left, after my mom was dropped off at the airfield, after Grandpa Amos left in the evening—I found my father on the couch. The TV was on, he was sleeping.

His crippled arm was bent under and behind him. Numb and limp, the hand grabbed at nothing. He was dreaming. His eyelids fluttered.

## 7

That summer he did handyman work. Laying wood floors mostly, which he managed one-armed. He took me with him every day after my mom left for the desert. He was supposed to drop me off at daycare but he didn't.

It was embarrassing at the daycare. I was too old to be there, even if it was summer break.

We rolled up to a blacktop driveway in his truck, some place in town, in Indianola, the front of a house painted in Crayola colors, an area to the side fenced in with chain-link where there were plastic slides, a sandbox, a basketball hoop with a metal net. Moms were dropping their kids off for the day. We sat in the truck and watched. Hugs and kisses. Moms with wet hair, in beige slacks. Moms in blouses and jackets on their way to work in Des Moines.

"I don't want to go," I told him.

He wouldn't get out of the truck and make me go inside. I knew he wouldn't.

He turned the engine over, cranked the column shifter into gear, and we left.

## 8

He had all the work he wanted in Urbandale and Merle Hay. Word of mouth spread across subdivision lines from woman to woman. Even with the one arm that didn't unbend he could still hold things in that hand, in a painful, shaky grip, if he angled his body to that side, or used scrap pieces to trap boards plumb against the chopsaw back. The women always wondered how he didn't lose a finger like that.

Sometimes he had me hold the board, even though my mom had told me to keep away from the saw. More often than not it was easier for my dad to hold the board himself.

I got him tools when asked. Hammer, shim, awl, punch, putty knife, belt sander. I carried him scraps of lumber. He yelled if I banged anything on the door molding (which is why he got full boards himself) or if I dropped something on the carpet, if it was new carpet.

He and my mom had renovated the house we lived in. It was the old house from the farm he grew up on.

I never knew my grandparents on his side. They died before I was born. The farmland partitioned off. The house had been unoccupied for some time when my parents came to fix it up. They met in Des Moines, where she went to nursing school. They tore out carpet and ripped down grease-saturated wallpaper, sanded the floors and crippled in new boards to replace the rotted ones. They scared rodents out of the attic, shot raccoons with a pellet gun. I sat to the side watching them stain the woodwork, or paste long strips of new wallpaper. I remember these things from the photos they took. It must have meant a lot to my father to keep his family in the farmhouse. To do all this even with a lame arm.

"What did grandpa die from?" I asked.

"There was a drunk driver." He winced, saying that. "It was him, you know. My dad. He'd been drinking and rolled the car. He and mom flew out and nobody could save them."

## 9

It was okay with him if I sat out of the way and banged on matchbox cars with the hammer. The carpet fiber was cool to my skin when I laid my face to it, in those houses where women ran the air conditioning all day.

These were stay-at-home women. A few divorced. They were always hanging around. Checking out the work. Complimenting my father on something technical or another they didn't know the right word for. They made lunch so we wouldn't have to leave for McDonald's. Meatloaf, roast beef, chicken casserole. Not just sandwiches—food that made it hard to finish the work in an afternoon. Sometimes they baked cookies or jelly-filled kolache, and hovered behind as we ate.

## 10

I never thought of my father as good-looking. His arm.

My mom was good-looking. She was different from everybody. Part Cleveland Jew, part Chicago Chicana. A Brasilian diplomat mixed in somewhere along the way, the relatives all swore, who took a bullet during a Chilean coup, and that's why he never returned from what was sworn to be a legitimate envoy to the Andes.

My father's line was mostly Germanic. It was linear. Comfortably Midwestern. Middle American, Central Iowan. His name? Ben Schmidt. He wore overalls when he worked and jeans when company came over. Sometimes he pronounced overalls *overhauls* to be funny, to make my mom and me smile, mocking the way the old-timers around there talked. But I think now he liked talking that way and wasn't always joking. It must have warmed him inside to say *Missour-uh* and *Ioway* and *Neebrasskee.*

## 11

My father was tall. He had light hair, a square jaw, a patchy beard that grew up his cheeks. The women he worked for didn't mind his lame arm. They seemed all the more interested once they heard the story of how he'd been hurt, the car accident, the drunk friend. "Hell. We were all drunk," he'd admit to a woman he was working for. She'd stare at his lame arm when he wasn't looking her direction, a woman would. She'd let her fingertips glance over the unmoving surface of his skin when he was done for the day, to see if he'd notice her touching him. Sweat and sawdust collected in the fine whitish hair of his forearms. Women tried to brush the sawdust away.

These strange women of the suburbs.

## 12

We were three weeks in the house of Trish Schumacher that July, out in Jordan Creek, where she lived by the mall, by a golf course and the cul-de-sac of a megachurch built up like a philistine temple in stucco.

Trish and her husband were loaded. Mr. Schumacher was a lawyer, or a minister, I don't remember. Trish was in real estate. They had a big new house. Big new cars with lots of chrome and showroom shine. Escalades.

Trish thought the finish work in the bathrooms was botched during the construction of her new house, so that's why she called my father. "I heard about this Ben Schmidt from my girlfriends," she said, "and I had to have him."

## 13

Trish liked to check on the work. She liked to appraise and laud, to ask dumb questions, to tell about some house she sold that year and its countertops.

Trish talked to me too. I was an easy target for women. My dark complexion, my near-white blond hair. Trish thought I was adopted the first day—she didn't know what my mom was like. I was scrawny. Like my dad, I wouldn't start really growing until high school.

## 14

When we were alone Trish asked me things. How I liked school. If I liked living on a farm. "Are there any kids out where you live? Some neighbor girl?" I shook my head. "I had two brothers and two sisters. A big family, me in the middle. Not too old, not too young," she laughed. "I think it's sad for an only child. Don't you think so? To not have anyone to play with."

She was just talking. I didn't even look at her. I sat cross-legged in the dry bathtub bottom, rolled matchbox cars until they were in a row.

She tapped her rings on the edge of the bathtub. "You don't have to tell me. I can imagine what it's like."

## 15

"Oscar is a tough nut to crack," my father said, back from the truck.

## 16

In the evening there were video calls with Mom. She was just getting up. Or just going to bed. I don't remember what time it would have been over there. She was tired.

My father dialed in the PC that sat on the floor next to the television, but he went outside before she answered. I brought the fishbowl downstairs to brag how I was keeping my goldfish alive.

She talked about the food she ate, once the PC was dialed in, the kinds of equipment she had around her neck and in the pockets of her med kit. Her stethoscope, her thermometer. Rubber gloves. Her voice digitized, sometimes doubling over itself in echoes. She always wore her hair up, over there, wore khaki tee shirts that fit tight around her. She smiled big when she saw me. So big the video broke up in pixilation. She asked how my day went and told me about her day. She tried to tell me about the people she worked with, or the bunker she rushed to if the Sense & Warn detected incoming, she said; and the geography, the mounds of desert that blew in under the doorways; and on the airplane going over, watching the sunset and sunrise only three hours apart over the Arctic Ocean.

I didn't hear any of that.

If she told me to shut up about asking when she was coming home, I would.

## 17

I told her what things my father did wrong around the house. I ratted him out for being unsafe around the saw, for letting me skip bath, for wearing the same shirt all week, for drinking too much beer, for the beard he was growing. (I didn't tell how we ate McDonald's for both lunch and dinner, for fear that this would mean the end of going to McDonald's.)

My father never did video call. Not that I saw. She wouldn't know what he was up to if I didn't tell her.

## 18

I told my mom about the women. When she said to shut up about her coming home, that she'd be back before I knew what, then I told about Trish Schumacher.

She listened quietly. She smiled, her face held fixed so that it looked like the signal was lost, her face on the screen vibrating, freezing, her eyes closed, as the satellite signal buffered and reset. "Oscar," she came back, "don't worry about any women. Tell him to put you in the daycare. The teacher knows you're coming. Okay? You will be happier there."

## 19

I returned the fishbowl to the desk in my bedroom after the call. Watched the fish gasp at the surface of the water for a while then fed him so he would stop. He only looked at me when he was hungry. Then he swam circles in the bowl.

I didn't know what a goldfish was supposed to do. The fish was doing it right, I figured.

## 20

My father built bonfires at night. I joined him if I couldn't sleep, if he was still out, and imagined what it would be like if Indianola, or our house, were bombed like the cities in the desert were bombed. When I looked to the house I saw flames reflect in the glass of my bedroom window. I imagined myself watching the fire from the window, except the fire was bombs.

My father made fires that were taller than he was. Four or five times a week.

There were a few acres of land we had, close to the highway spur. A copse of cottonwood, a few burr oaks with craggy veins of bark as thick as my arm.

He had a pole saw. A serrated blade at the end of bamboo. He pruned trees one-armed, the pole handle wedged in his armpit. He cut out dead wood and tossed it on the pile. Raked up the leaves and debris his cutting made and dropped that in the flames too. The idea of burning up part of the world must have appealed to him. Soothed him, or stoked his discomfort. I'm not sure which. He took something solid, a log, a branch, and with a simple chemical procedure watched it turn to gas and vapor, something that rose weightless and dispersed into the atmosphere. Something that blew away.

## 21

**W**e drove to the daycare in the morning. He said to get out. I didn't want to. "You got to take me in," I told him. "Or I won't go."

The children scrambled around the playground. One of the women who worked there was slicing watermelon for them. The children who could sit still bit into their slices and chewed. They rubbed their mouths with the backs of their hands, slime from the melon dripping down their chins. When they were done the woman wiped their faces with a stained white rag.

## 22

**"F**ollow this way," Trish said. "There's something I want to show you. You'll like this."

She led outside and across the patio to the garage. Grasshoppers launched out of our way, into wet, matted grass that smelled of mildew. "Do you like tractors?" she asked. "Farmboys always like tractors."

In the corner behind her white and gold Escalade was a riding lawnmower, a bright green John Deere with a yellow blade deck. It looked like a miniature tractor.

Trish grabbed my hand and heaved me to the cushion. Told me to take the wheel.

"See how you look up there? Just perfect. A little farmer."

She wore a skirt and a glittery, sleeveless blouse. She crouched when she talked. Her knees came up and I saw. I could see along her leg, under the skirt.

I thought of the times Trish excused herself. How in the morning she wore yoga pants and a sports bra, like that morning, then changed in the room next to where my father worked. I heard Trish rattle open drawers, bang the top on a hamper. She unclicked the spring lock on the door but didn't come out changed, not for a minute or two.

I wanted to see. This bloviating woman in the short skirt. I wanted to see her underwear, the rose and pink, I saw, the swell of thigh up to where silk flashed.

"We had plenty of fun on tractors and in the backs of trucks when I was a girl," she said. "Do you believe I grew up on a farm too? Of course you don't."

Trish told her 4-H stories, her cheerleading stories, her drive-in movie stories, her Wartburg College stories. Her breasts swung as she gestured to make a *W* with her arms. Her blouse hung open as she leaned close. "Promise you won't tell your dad what I told you. This stuff makes me sound like a dinosaur."

She had me there looking down her shirt at the tanned cleavage flesh.

She plucked the key from the Deere's ignition to examine it.

"Do you miss your mom?" she asked. "I couldn't have left my kids like that. Mine aren't kids anymore, but still. You must miss her something awful."

## 23

**I** was happy when Trish left me on the lawnmower and went inside. It was over, I thought, what she was putting me through. I bounced on the seat cushion and turned the wheel from side to side, listened to the rubber tires squeal on the synthetic garage surface. It was boring, but I didn't want to go in the house. I looked around the garage, curious because it was clean and new. The garages I knew had a layer of oil grunge on the ground, their walls lined with drowsy fireflies, orange and black wings folded, because there was a gap under the door that let in bugs. But there were no bugs in the Schumacher garage. No oil spots. The floor was painted blue. It smelled like nothing really, nothing I could identify or remember.

I thought about my mom. Her dark hair, long and curly. The orange irises of her eyes. She was comfortable in uniforms. She'd played sports in high school. She was a nurse and the Guard needed nurses. That's how she ended up serving in the desert. That's why she joined the Guard, anyway, for the bonus, for the salary, to help out when floods hit Iowa, when tornadoes spun through. She had no idea she'd be shipped off to the Middle East. She had no clue what was coming, or that the President would make the militia fight foreign wars.

I was upset, most of the time, I realize now. I almost never spoke a word to anyone except my father then, and am still quiet compared to most. People mention this when they meet me. I shrug, unable to explain.

I knew they'd bury her body with others, if something happened. They'd drop her lifeless in the sand. If she died there. I'd seen it happen on the news my father watched. The shows on cable he fell asleep to on the couch.

If she died so far from home, I wondered, would she go to Heaven? If she did go to Heaven, would she remember me?

## 24

**H**e was out by the bonfire later, dragging over a tree limb to segment and burn. I went to help him pull the limb across the dirt and he let me. He let me hold a branch as he sawed. It flopped up and down with the blade of the handsaw otherwise and he couldn't get it.

He talked to the fire. He didn't look at me.

"She sends e-mails all the time. Your mom. Tells me what life's going to be like once she gets back from Iraq. The three of us going to live as vagabonds, she says. Hitchhiking, living on the road. Gypsies. Going to see everything worth a damn that can be seen for free. We'll get a TV show and move to Hollywood, she says. Then she changes her mind. She's going to be a waitress in New York. No. We'll rent out paddle boats to tourists in Pensacola. She's come up with at least a dozen of them. Army jobs in Germany. Resorts in Costa Rica."

I never saw this side of my mom. She was practical and tough in front of me. But I don't doubt such impulses existed within her.

"I don't know," my father said. "What would possess a woman to think like that?"

He spit in the fire and waited.

"What's so wrong with what we got here?" he said. "We live and live. Nothing will change. That's what I tell her. We had a good life when she left."

## 25

The McDonald's was next to a gas station by the highway, across from the Walmart. There were mostly old farmers there for breakfast, who were there every morning in their patched jeans and Carhartts, their freebie seed company hats, to joke around and drink coffee and hassle the lady who managed the McDonald's, who took their teasing in good nature. Some of the farmers chatted up my father after we ordered. They knew my family. Some had probably volunteered on the rescue squad that responded to the crash that killed my grandparents. The farmers asked my father how the house was holding up, if he had enough work to keep him busy.

## 26

We sat in the truck in the daycare driveway. Kids were playing in the yard. The same kids as before, that had been eating the watermelon. We'd been here enough, sitting in the truck watching, that I recognized them.

They watched to see what would happen. I suppose they recognized us too, my father's truck at least. Maybe it was confusing for them when he got out and came to my side to open the door and lifted me with his good arm and set me on the blacktop. How we stopped at the gate and waited to see what would happen next, because we didn't know how drop-off was supposed to be done. Who my father should talk to. If he needed to sign a book or what.

A woman came to meet us. Her name was Miss Stephanie. She asked if I was Oscar, and my father said I was. Perfect, she said. They'd been waiting for me, she said.

The sports bar waitress was named Kim Boettcher. She was a blonde and had a soft round stomach she liked to show off. She wore her jeans low on her hips. Aaron met her outside a grocery store, where her bank was. They were parked next to each other and she rapped on his window to complain after he took her photo. She had on the apron she kept her tips in at work.

"You can't do that," Kim told him. She wanted to be a broadcast journalist and enlightened him on consent laws. Aaron was happy to listen.

She lived with a couple friends in a south Omaha duplex. It was a single-story house with four garage doors on the street side. Her room was in the back, with a washer and dryer in the closet. Aaron slept there for three days.

Kim lay facedown while he massaged her with baby oil every morning, her eyes closed. When he put his weight on her body, Aaron could smell fryer grease in the sheets.

## The Current State of the Universe

It may seem funny to you, if you have a sense of justice, that someone in the etiquette-revenge business has had such a hard time in life—that so much has gone wrong for a man who's merely tried to make things right. I can't apologize for my career choice, however. It's simply what I'm good at.

This job is not taken in any conventional way, but, since you're here training now, you probably know that already. Our recruitment officers operate in county jail cells and detox tanks, seeking out petty vandals of government property and adventurous drunks. The point of our business is to make the ill-mannered aware of how it feels to be treated poorly. It's the little guy—the overweight, retarded, crippled, or flat-chested—that we protect with our work. What we do is teach people lessons on karma by fucking up their property.

If you've ever heard of something similar to the following, trust me, we're already operating in your city.

Maybe they told you all this in orientation, maybe they didn't. I'm going to tell you anyway. First, maybe you yell something out your car window at a guy on the sidewalk. *Keep walking, fatty* or *Screw you, asshole.* Or maybe just some filthy words to a beautiful young woman, something that seems innocent enough. Well, this person may be one of our clients or, even worse for you, one of our employees. Getting revenge is a simple process for them, merely a matter of writing down your license plate number and calling in a request for reparations. Through our contacts in the DMV we find out where you live. The next morning your taillights have been smashed out and half-inch lag screws have been drilled into your tires. It's simple. You cut someone off in traffic, flip them the bird, and in the morning the gate is open and your dog has run away. It isn't a coincidence. It's us. We're the Furies of the modern world—the vengeance of a god gone corporate.

This can be a nasty profession, don't get me wrong, but we do try to be cordial—breaking out the big windows when possible, which tend to be cheaper to replace, and doing pro bono work for low-income clients during the holiday season. Having a sense of propriety is important to our overall success. Even so, things haven't worked out for me as well as a man in the karma industry would hope. A big part of this job is having faith that the world is better because of us, that we must sometimes act against humanity in order to preserve a state of equilibrium. But occasionally a case goes so obviously wrong that it calls the whole system into question.

It gets me thinking, if karma is a real force, then maybe this line of work has been responsible for much of the misfortune that surrounds my life, for the accidents that mar my existence. After all, there's a history of others paying for my mistakes.

My era of uncertainty began with a typical case. A client was nearly run over as she crossed the street. The driver saw her, made eye contact, but the car kept moving. The Big Man (the CEO of Make Things Right Inc.) called me personally from corporate headquarters in White Plains because this woman was an important client. "We need this done right," he said. "You're our number one guy in the Midwest, the dark prince of the Plains, and no one takes a dump in that city of yours without asking us first. Make it happen!"

The Big Man was a motivational speaker from New Jersey in his former life and tended to err on the side of exaggeration, but I understood he demanded results. Having toiled in the hospitality industry for fifteen years prior to working for MTR, I knew all about the expectations upper management has for its mercenaries.

This is why I performed a thorough job on the car. I parked nearly a mile away, under a ponderosa pine, positioning my vehicle with an escape route in mind. Ponderosas are one of the best trees to hide a car under because their low branches are rarely trimmed and their needles grow in large, thick bursts. Weeping willows are good too, but are seldom planted near a curb. In this line of work it's important to notice these things. Like anything you love, the job allows you to really see the world around you, to look for every advantage, because you want to be the best there is.

This assignment was easy though. A car parked in a garage. Suburbanites are psychologically incapable of locking the back and side doors of their garages—as if that would be the final proof society had gone down the tubes. Once inside, I slashed his tires—a rasp probe jammed and withdrawn four times in a quick hissing minute—shattered his windows near silently with a spring-loaded pin designed by EMTs, and, finally, rubbed dog shit into the upholstery. This may seem harsh, but it's a shock-and-awe kind of thing. Our clients demand results and we do our utmost to satisfy them.

The problem in this case was that the car I vandalized didn't belong to the punk we were supposed to get. Whether the car was borrowed or the paperwork botched I don't know for sure, but the car belonged to a nice old man—a veteran of foreign wars active in the community and his church. After I messed up the car a local news station ran a story on his pathetic condition, this diabetic widower living on a fixed income. He couldn't make it to the doctor's office or to Sunday services. It was depressing to think about an old man stuck at home, waiting for a church mother to pick him up, because his late-model Pontiac had been vandalized.

This was a major error, something that wouldn't be forgotten within the company. And what's worse, in the coming weeks it seemed that this mistake was part of a bigger system, a network of checks and balances working to cut me down to size because of everything I'd done. In this line of work it's impossible to believe in coincidences. Even more than that, it's against company policy.

**A** week later, arms loaded with cleaning supplies, I arrived at the old man's house to make amends. It was morning, a mid-August day. The Big Man had called me earlier, spitting vitriol. It was my assignment to arrange a cleanup. In a bigger city, a crew with professional grease monkeys would have been called in, but the operation in Nebraska was streamlined. I often pulled double-duty.

The Pontiac was pretty much as I'd left it, although it had been rolled into the driveway by then, like the old man had tried to drive it to the shop himself, flat tires be damned, then thought better of it mid-act. Slumped in front of his split-level, vinyl-sided house, the car had garbage bags taped over its windows. It was easy to peel off the plastic and reach inside to flip the lock. I scrubbed his seats with a soapy brush to free the same dog shit I'd so enthusiastically smeared in a week before. A glass guy met me there and began work on the windows, pulled off the door consoles to vacuum out the green squares of shattered glass.

The old man scrutinized us from behind his screen door but didn't come outside. His finger was on the lock, his skinny legs peeking through a yellow robe. The squinty look reminded me of my own father, a small-town minister who never trusted me. I waved to the old man from the driveway. I had muscular arms and dirty-blond hair with an untamed cowlick spiking at the hairline. But I wasn't a frightening figure by any means.

"How do you do?" I offered my hand on the outer side of the screen door but he didn't budge. The old man was bald on top, with feathery white hair horseshoed from big ear to big ear. His blue eyes narrowed behind silver-rimmed glasses.

"Who are you?" he asked.

I smiled. "A mutual acquaintance said someone messed up your car. I'm here to fix it."

"You're from the church?"

"Not exactly."

The old man looked me up and down before rattling open the lock. "You're welcome to coffee, if you want it."

It took most of the morning to get the car into shape. The glass man was finished in an hour, but it was a bigger job to put the car on blocks, lever off his flat tires and shuttle them to the nearest auto shop to be patched. Lamb's-wool seat covers would obscure the stains, and three shampoo and rinse cycles eliminated the smell. It felt good to engage in this kind of labor, honestly, working in the sunshine instead of lurking in the damp hours of early morning.

Around lunchtime the old man came outside to inspect the work. He kicked the wet-black tires and leaned into the car to sniff the Armor All'd dashboard.

"Still don't know who sent you," he said, "but may God bless you for coming."

"It's no trouble, mister. Really. Just something that had to be done."

He looked me in the eyes, pained resignation on his face, like he had something to tell me that couldn't be said politely.

"I wonder if you'd let me know who did this," he said.

"That wouldn't be right," I tried to explain, packing my supplies. "But you should know that they're sorry. It wasn't personal."

"Does that make it better? That it wasn't personal?"

I told myself that this was just my job, these things I did. Make Things Right was a corporation like any other.

"No," I said, splashing a bucket of dirty water toward his grass. "I don't think it does make it any better."

After loading the gear into the back of my truck I shook the old man's hand. He was so affable—wrinkled and saggy in his cardigan. I'd known dozens of men like him in my father's church, growing up. Men I sometimes felt nostalgic for, even though I'd done nothing but terrorize them when I was young.

"If you need anything, let me know."

"I will," the old man said. He hung around my truck, hands in his pockets. "If you're looking for more of this kind of work, I know a group that helps people."

"A charity?"

I must have sounded dubious, or offended, because he reassured me it wasn't a church.

"They help out those who can't help themselves. People who have no one else."

"We'll see," I said.

Maybe it sounds strange, but I'd never really considered nonprofit work before. Several of our agents had quit during that time to go into the charity industry, but the work we did was just as good as any NPO's as far as I was concerned.

"Call this number." The old man handed me a business card. "Frank is a friend."

"Sure." I slid the card into my shirt pocket without looking at it. "If you need anything. Dinner? Groceries? I can get it for you."

"Call the number," he said, then he turned to his house.

It wasn't even three weeks later that the old man died. The lug nuts weren't torqued tight enough, or were too tight, and had come free. A wheel wiggled loose while he drove and shot from the car; there was nothing the old man could do to stop from hitting a light pole. This too was on the news, a good Samaritan's act of kindness gone wrong because the idiot didn't know how to tighten a lug nut. Nothing special, really, if I wasn't the idiot in this particular instance.

It didn't take long, after hearing of his demise, to call the number the old man had given me. I was uneasy with the knowledge that my negligence had killed someone. I feared that my mere presence in the world was toxic. (My parents had also been killed in a car accident, I should let you know, although their deaths had nothing in common with the old man's. This was six years earlier. Their car was run off a county highway by a semi loaded with sugar beets. These things happen. There was nothing weird in the way they died, except that they were my parents, for one, and that I was a lifelong fuckup, for another. But maybe there's nothing weird about that either. Maybe that's exactly the way it was supposed to happen.)

They called themselves the Coalition Against Poverty, *Citizens dedicated to improving the experience of the poverty-stricken and destitute.* It seemed meaningful that the old man had given me this card. Like maybe this could be free-range karma at work, the universe struggling to repair itself. This guy Frank answered my call and we set up a meeting.

CAP's office was near downtown, in a decimated corridor off Zero Street that housed other charities and liquor stores. The area was familiar to me, a district of last vestiges, of architectural relics and human remnants. Their office was nice though. The interior was newly apportioned and restored, with shined furniture and red brick walls that looked original. It smelled like carpet adhesive, the way most offices do. In my past life as a corporate slob I'd been made to wait in a hundred lobbies like this one—in fluorescent mini-malls, in downtown skyscrapers, in reapportioned warehouses.

After filling out a packet of information I was shown to Frank's office in the back of the building. Taking a seat, I apologized for calling on a Saturday.

"Not a problem." Frank was a large man, thick through the shoulders and chest. He wore a worn-out shirt and tie. "As you can imagine, Saturday is a busy day for volunteers."

"Makes sense."

"Yours is an intriguing résumé," Frank said. He flipped through my papers. "Impressive business credentials. Management training. Bachelor's degree." Frank sat at his desk in a catcher's stance, his chair low to the ground, his knees up, hands open in front of his chest, ready to block any junk I could throw at him. "But nothing in the last five years," he noted. "Did you win the lottery, Mr. Dandrow?"

"I haven't been in prison, if that's what you're implying."

"No, no. We will have to run a background check, though. We can't accept felons."

"That won't be a problem," I told him. Make Things Right had cleansed my record as part of its SOP.

"Let me cut the shit," Frank said, looking up from his desk. "I have a pretty strong notion why you showed up today.

We get a lot of your type in here, wanting to make amends for something horrible they've done."

"Maybe you don't want me. My past is pretty ugly. The things I've done could be shocking to someone like you."

"Don't try to gaslight me. I know who you've been working for. We're well aware of MTR and the things they do." He rocked back in his chair, letting his hands settle on his gut as he stared at me for a moment, biting his lower lip. "You know, the Romans believed the Furies were a self-cursing phenomenon. Whoever summoned them also ended up getting fucked over in the end. It was their way of saying that revenge doesn't work."

It must have surprised me, what Frank said, because he motioned that I should stay seated. I didn't think anyone knew about Make Things Right. Who would really believe there was a company doing what we did? It was easier to conceive of randomness, of teenagers up to no good, than to envision a corporate entity in the business of revenge.

"No," he said. "I don't care what kind of work you did before. CAP needs talented people, wherever they come from. If you like to dabble in karma, we can help with that too." He turned his back to me and walked to the window behind his desk. There wasn't much of a view beyond the glass. Just a chain-link fence, a parking lot behind it. "I was pretty damn good at shooting people when I was in the Marines, but it didn't become my life's work. It only matters what you do from now on. That's what you're judged by."

Frank didn't need to convince me. I was ready to help. If I wanted to do good in the world, why not take a straight path instead of trying to navigate the inequities of revenge. Things had gone poorly with the old man, but there were plenty of good deeds that could be done in this city. Groceries needed delivering. Gardens needed weeding. Motor oil needed changing. I was the man for the work, so that's what I told him.

I started the next day, spent six hours trimming back a cancer patient's overgrown yard. She watched me from the window as her flowering shrubs came back into view after an hour of yanking native grass and milkweed from her garden.

I wasn't great at gardening, but, with charity work, it was the thought that counted, right? I waved happily to the woman's neighbors as I walked behind a humming mower, and at the end of the day, it felt good to look back on the progress I'd made. This was something I always loved about revenge work too, the instant gratification of seeing a job well done. The crisp green lines left by a lawn mower, the metallic squiggles etched into a keyed car. The difference was that with charity work, fleeing wasn't necessary. I could stay and see the satisfied expression of the person whose property I'd altered. We could drink iced tea together.

"It looks so nice," the woman said as we sat on her porch. Her name was Jill. She was wheelchair-bound, in her early forties, her head wrapped in a blue scarf. To my surprise, she reached for my hand and brought it to her face to kiss my dirt-stained knuckles.

"The weeds will stay away for a while now," I said, pulling my hand back.

"Till spring." She slouched in her wheelchair. "Let's hope I can pull them myself then."

I did hope that, for the hour we sat on her porch. I was nearly praying, to be honest, contemplating how her life would be better from then on, because of my actions, rather than in spite of them.

Frank sent me to assist all sorts of people in the following weeks. Victims of gang violence who were helpless and alone, living in bad neighborhoods; migrants injured on the job; kids with HIV. I cleared gutters for the elderly and clumsy, weatherproofed windows for the single mothers of thin-blooded children, installed lift chairs for the morbidly obese. I paid bills, delivered meals-on-wheels, cleared basements of sagging boxes. I collected toys for tots and recyclables for the rag-and-can men living in the park. For those first couple months I was a revelation to myself and others. These acts of restitution felt like a blanket over the city.

But things didn't always go so well. There was the strange case of Jimmy Motts, for instance. His was a nuanced example, someone Frank regarded as his brightest success story, or at least a man who had such potential. Motts had come to CAP as a OxyContin addict years before and progressed through their programs in a drawn-out cycle of relapse and recovery. By the time I met him he was a part-time employee of CAP, driving around doing audits of volunteer work. He still received benefits, however, because he was only partially recovered.

I mowed his lawn and did garden work. Jill had given me high marks for my landscaping efforts, and this would have been an easy job too if it weren't for Motts sitting on the porch offering a glib critique. He was a boxy man and had a letter-jacket pride he wore in his shoulders and jaw. It was a hot day, and he drank light beer, reclining on his steps to point out spots I'd missed by jabbing his finger toward a stray dandelion or a stubborn patch of crabgrass. Even though Motts was on methadone, he had a live-in girlfriend and a nice truck. I hadn't had a girl in years, and my truck was a piece of shit. It seemed to me that Motts was running a con on CAP.

When I was about to leave Motts stood and came to offer a final assessment. "You need to pull that," he said, indicating a plant with a big mustard-yellow bloom that I'd left in the middle of his garden.

"That's a flower," I said.

"Jesus Christ," he murmured. "Don't you know anything? It's ragweed."

"Ragweed?" I strolled over to nudge the plant stalk with the tip of my shoe. It wasn't an unattractive flower, but he was apparently right. My nose started to run, as if to spite me.

"Yes," he started again. "Ragweed. Weed, as in it's a noxious plant."

I pulled the plant out by its roots and held it up so he could see the root tendrils sprinkle dirt on his sidewalk. "It's gone now."

"You're Dandrow, aren't you?"

"That's right."

"Of course," he said. "That explains the shit job you did."

"What did you say?"

"That you being James Dandrow explains the shoddy work."

I said, "Screw you," and walked toward my truck. It didn't matter what this guy said. I was going to leave, but Motts followed.

He was delusional, thinking he could spook me. If he knew what business I was in he wouldn't have acted like that. What was he going to do to me that I couldn't do back to him tenfold? It was like a gym teacher trying to sell protection to the mob.

"I can make things rough for you," I warned him. "You don't want to mess with me."

"Fuck that." He laughed. "I'm not done with you."

"Then hit me," I snapped, taking a step toward him. Motts pushed me, but I bucked against him with my chest and yelled again. "Hit me!"

He reared back, loading up for a haymaker, and while I waited for his fist, he lurched forward and struck me square in the chest with his forehead. At that moment I understood this man was not well.

Both of us were dazed—Motts because of the head trauma, me because I was so baffled by what had just happened. His barrage of complaints had made me forget myself. For a moment I'd wanted to take revenge on him, surely I had. In those seconds, a reflex, my brain mapped out his property and calculated an appropriate amount of punishment to mete out.

I wasn't going to do this, of course, merely because this crazy man had insulted me. Even though it felt counterintuitive at the time, I knew that the mentally ill hardly ever deserved to get punched.

By this time his girlfriend had come out on the porch. "Jimmy," she called, her hands on the banister as she leaned toward us. Motts was sitting on the sidewalk then, rubbing the shape out of his hair, blinking.

"I'm leaving," I said. I climbed into my truck.

"No," he shouted. He crawled into a teetering squat to face me. "Don't!"

Motts couldn't back down, even though the fight had ended.

"This isn't over, you pussy. You didn't even throw a punch."

Somehow, even as I drove away, I knew I'd soon be back.

**W**hen I'm alone at night I often think of sitting with my parents in the living room of their old house. We talk about world news and debate theology, but it's an imaginary dialogue. My parents never sat together on the couch like that, engaging me in their pleasant conversation, no matter how much it eases my mind to pretend they did.

In the fantasy my dad sits with his legs crossed, a look of unyielding compassion on his face. He says, "Get with it, son. Take off out of here."

He's wearing a sharp outfit, neutral colors. My mother's hair is done beautifully. The soft smell of her lotion fills the room.

"You're smart," she says. "Make an honest impression on people."

These dreams hold appeal for me now, they always have, and they surely did in the days I volunteered with CAP. I thought about the ways my life could have been different, if only we'd known the right things to say to each other, me and my parents.

I'm from the dust-bowl part of Nebraska, near McCook, the only child of an Episcopalian minister. My childhood was a chaotic one, filled with self-incriminations and crimes of passion. Everyone knew I was a wild kid, but my father had it in his mind that he could keep me in check.

"Satan isn't in you," he'd reassure me, holding my shoulders. "It's just a restlessness. God has a plan for you."

It hadn't yet occurred to me that I was possessed by the devil. Sure, there were things I'd done. Tasteless pranks. More than a few dramatic flashes of brattiness in front of relatives and neighbors. But they didn't matter much in the grand scheme of things. They weren't evil acts.

The real trouble started after I left for college. A string of MIPs and DUIs followed my initiation into a fraternity. My grades were adequate, but my moral certitude was flagging. My father was a strong believer of so-called small-town values. He suggested that maybe the state capital, or a libertine school, wasn't the best place for me, that I should come home. But I didn't agree and was eighteen years old. It was important I learned to stay out of trouble on my own, I insisted, then remained in school.

It wasn't until eight years later that I saw my father again. He bulged around the middle, but the rest of him was sickly, thin, weak from worry, I thought. He was bald, with just a few wisps of red hair around the sides of his head and a sparse mustache.

At the time, my career in corporate hospitality was hanging by a thread, my whole life edifice. I had a job with a good sound to it, but no real money to my name. Nice clothes, but a dirty, one-room apartment behind a Szechuan restaurant. I was living in the student district of Lincoln, which was a major mistake, looking back. If I'd wanted to remain employed, partying six nights a week with undergrads was a poor decision. But I don't regret it. The past doesn't work that way. Your whole life is tied together; if one string is pulled, others are going to come with it.

My father summoned me home that summer because he heard a rumor from one of his parishioners about a certain McCook girl. This gossip had the stain of sexual misdeed. A freshman coed tricked into dangerous situations by an older man, plied with alcohol, and, eventually, shuttled to an abortion clinic. I've forgotten some of the things he accused me of, but they were all true. She was a student at Wesleyan, a confused thing when I found her. A hippie redneck invested in tie-dye tee shirts, hemp purses, and cowboy hats. I never saw her again.

When he cornered me on it, I told my father that I would never again embarrass him, something neither of us believed.

"Why can't you treat women right?" he kept asking. "Why can't you treat anyone the way *you* want to be treated?"

On this point the pastor didn't understand me—I was trying to live by that creed.

It was true I'd been a bastard to just about everyone I knew, but life wasn't exactly kind to me in those years either. My job was beyond saving, even if I'd cared to keep it. My car had been repossessed. My shitty apartment remained the same. Later, there was the car crash that took my parents. (This was my harshest failure, my parents' deaths—the one that cut closest to my murmuring heart. Do you understand what I mean? I think you do.) I sought out hardship and easily found it, going from one troubled woman to another, unable to love. I was a starvation artist, a masochist, which was okay, so long as it didn't hurt anybody else. The problem was that I couldn't control the flow of misfortune. It spread all around me.

Three years later the Big Man discovered me in detox. He did his own recruiting in those fledgling days, lurking in the dark corner of my cell. He was still a young man then, in a gray suit with a silver tie, his hair moussed over his big Italian skull. His was a voice I could listen to. I'd been on a long meandering drunk since my parents died, and MTR offered a job that built character in a certain way. Perhaps I was weak when he found me, or maybe it was restlessness, as my father once believed. Whatever the reason, I accepted his proposal. What the Big Man told me was irresistible—that any man who doesn't pursue his salvation will find only ruin. This was my chance to atone for my misdeeds.

MTR was a family business at the time, a dozen of us across four noncontiguous states. The Big Man trained each of us personally, took us to hardware stores to purchase the tools of our trade, stayed for a month's worth of assignments to demonstrate how revenge work was properly done, accompanied us to twelve-step meetings, and then let us loose to do the job we'd been charged with. He allowed me to throw myself into the work, to mask my grief by burying it in the misfortune of others.

**N**ot long after the incident with Jimmy Motts, Frank called me into his office. He was crouched at his desk with a hand half-covering his face, the worn tie dangling between his knees.

"I hate to say it, Dandrow, but you might not be cut out for this kind of work."

I sat across from him and tried to see what was written in the file he read from.

"There are troubling reports," he explained. "There are complaints."

"Was I rude to someone?"

"No, it wasn't rudeness. They all think you're a peach of a person. Not sure how you did *that*, but whatever. If they like you, I can like you too. I appreciate what you're trying to do."

I didn't understand what he was saying and feared it had to do with my past, with MTR or something surrounding the estate of the old man, a lawsuit. It was almost winter then. His office was dark in the weak morning light.

"This isn't easy to say. You're bad at charity work."

He seemed like he wanted to laugh at the absurdity but was resolved not to. His face red from the strain. Frank may not have liked me, but that's a funny thing to have to tell someone.

"Your heart is there, I believe, but the particulars don't happen for you."

"What do you mean?"

"Mrs. Keen's gutters, for example. When you cleaned them, you kicked loose some shingles. She then had a leaky roof."

"Is that true? I can fix it next—"

Frank held up a meaty finger. "The lift chair you found for Mr. Hanson, it had a short circuit, almost started a fire. When you cleared those boxes out of the Sedlak basement, did you notice black mold? That stuff is toxic. Had it been sucked into the ventilation they'd of been goners."

My chest felt heavy. All I could manage to say was, "Jeez."

"There's more." Frank held up a stack of bound pages. "But I'll spare you the details. We both know why you're here."

"Jimmy Motts."

"That's right. Jimmy Motts."

"Did he tell you that he rammed my chest with his forehead?"

"He told me that you provoked him, that—"

"C'mon, Frank. You don't believe that bullshit, do you?"

"I don't have to. Your record speaks for itself."

"But there's the woman whose garden I fixed. She'll vouch for me."

"Jill's dead," Frank replied. "She passed last week."

I recalled the visage of that now-dead woman, and I questioned myself again.

"Was Motts the auditor on these jobs?"

"Now, don't start that woe-is-me shit. You knew the rules when you started. With your background, the one thing you absolutely couldn't do was confront a client." Frank leaned forward, set his jaw in his hands. "Not everyone we help is a kind-hearted old lady. Sometimes they're crazy. Sometimes they're maniacs who probably deserve to get hit. I know that.

But it's our job to help them all. Each and every one of them. We don't get to pick, okay? How we come to meet these people, how they come to my office, it's beyond me. But that's the point, isn't it? It's not up to us."

Frank stood and walked to the door. As he opened it I could hear the receptionist arguing with someone on the phone.

"We love your effort," Frank said, holding out his hand. "But I can't give you any more jobs. Not after all this." He whispered this last part, pointing toward the folder. "It would be a PR disaster. You've worked in corporate. You can understand that."

**N**o one likes to be fired, particularly from a volunteer position, but as I left Frank's office that day a sense of relief flickered within me. Honestly, it was a little disarming to work in the daylight, to be welcomed into someone's home. People let me play catch with their children. I was handed a baby girl once, despite my protestations, embarrassed that I didn't know how to hold her. It seemed like a mistake when a woman wanted to hug me after I raked her leaves, when her children smiled shyly to reveal lost teeth, saying, "Thanky, Mister James."

This wasn't part of the world I knew. Even if these people accepted me, it didn't mean I belonged there, defrosting their refrigerators.

They said I was a model citizen, some of them. Don't get me wrong, I knew how full of shit they were. I was still working with Make Things Right at night, of course. I had to get paid somehow. The people I helped with CAP didn't know how I'd shattered over a hundred windshields, slashed sixty sets of tires, scarred the bark of hundred-year-old family oak trees, stuck cockle burrs in people's tube socks, set free beloved family pets, and planted child pornography on an elementary school teacher's home computer—or that this chicanery had paid my bills and taxes. I wondered what they would think of me if they found out.

In many ways the incident that led to my being let go by Citizens Against Poverty was a fortuitous one. It seemed that there were many revolutions to the ups and downs a man must face. No matter what kind of life he's living, not everything will turn up roses—especially not for a guy who tempts fate like Jimmy Motts.

The fact that we're at his house now is a case in point. Some people won't believe this is a coincidence. Maybe you're one of those people. For you, this is just a simple training exercise, but it means a lot more to me. The universe offers second chances to those open to receiving them. I know this.

Believe me, I don't hold a grudge against Motts. I'm a professional—there's no need to recuse myself. He flipped off an old woman in traffic, defamed God in front of her grandkids. That's why we're here. We'll wait as long as it takes, even if Motts is up most of the night, lingering in one room or another, snacking in the kitchen, brushing his teeth. When the lights are doused we'll be ready.

Maybe it's true what Frank said about the Furies being a self-reflexive phenomenon—that to invoke their powers is to curse yourself—but I don't care anymore. It's who I am.

We may not be able to meddle in fate, of this I'm fairly certain—but it's also true that we can't pick our talents. This is the difference between a job and a vocation. Some people just go to work and wait it out till payday. But some of us, people like me, we'd do this stuff for free.

---

He introduced himself to Carrie Rehbein at a karaoke bar by the freeway. She was from Ashland and had come to Omaha that day to go shopping with her sisters. She had green eyes and red hair, wore a tight yellow tee shirt under her coat and two small gold necklaces around her neck. Her engagement had been broken off the month before, just after Thanksgiving, her sisters said.

It was obvious her sisters were the ones who really wanted Carrie to go home with Aaron. All of them drank tumblers of white wine.

The sisters sang raunchy lyrics they'd improvised over karaoke versions of Mariah Carey and Shania Twain, until the DJ refused to let them go on again. They got Carrie too drunk to drive home and made Aaron promise he'd take care of her.

Carrie was nervous to be alone with him, once they were in her car. She turned and looked out the window, watching for her sisters as he drove her away.

# Attend the Way

It's because he has a train to catch that Rodney leaves his room after suppertime. He puts on dress shoes and his green suit, the one that looks good against his skin. Earlier that afternoon, the big woman next door trimmed his hair. He lives in the Kellogg Rooming House, an old brick building near downtown. It's a fifteen-block walk to the train station from his room and he wants to arrive early. It's a nice evening, the lights of the big buildings downtown popping on. Rodney heads south to Leavenworth. He knows a few people on the street here but doesn't stop to talk. He doesn't even care when the boys he knows laugh at him for wearing a suit.

A pair of granite buildings sit on the Tenth Street hilltop. Each of them used to be central stations for rail lines at one time, but the one that's bright and clean is a museum now and the other sits empty, its exterior smog-gray and mossy-green, *The Burlington Station* etched at its top. The Amtrak station is a small brick building nestled in a depression behind these old giants. Rodney's headed for Hastings, a town some hundred-fifty miles away. It will be two in the morning when he arrives. He'd have rented a car if he had a driver's license and a credit card, but he doesn't have these things. It's either the train or a bus for a man with only paper ID and a clip of small bills, and you won't catch Rodney riding a bus.

He'll spend as little time as possible in Hastings—his mother's died there, that's the reason he's going—and then he'll take the train coming home to Omaha.

When Rodney wakes up he's slumped cockeyed in his seat, leaning against a young man who plunked next to him at the stop in Lincoln. It takes Rodney a moment to realize where he's at, to lift his head off that shoulder and straighten, to remember he's on a train in the middle of nowhere, in the middle of the night. "Good morning," the young man says. Rodney doesn't respond. He merely rubs his face and looks out the window. The young man smiles, he laughs softly. "Have you come a long way?" he asks.

Rodney angles his body to the window so the kid will stop talking.

The train is due to arrive at two a.m. and as far as Rodney knows it's on time. This must be Hastings, he thinks, the train slowing into town. Even though his mother grew up here and had been living at the Medicaid home for years, Rodney has never been to Hastings before. Neither had his father, who died years ago. There isn't much for Rodney to see out the window. Some houses and rectangular brick buildings, long lonely streets with cars parked here and there, faintly lit plastic signs marking off businesses that are closed for the night. It's mid-summer and even in the bluish darkness of early morning things look yellow and dry.

Rodney waits on a bench after getting off the train because he doesn't know where to go. A few others deboard with him, but they have people waiting for them, folks they blearily embrace, somnambulists who help load luggage into the back of a car and then drive off. By the time the train chugs off toward its next stop the station is quiet again, save for the shuffling of Rodney's feet and the young man he sat by earlier talking on a cell phone.

When the young man closes his phone and slides it into his pocket, Rodney approaches him, slowly, because he doesn't want to risk scaring the kid. "Do you know how to find this place?" He hands the young man a slip of paper with the nursing home's address on it. It was his girl who told him about his mother, because her place was Rodney's last known address. There was a message from his girl in the office at the Kellogg one day, after Rodney went back to the rooming house, telling about his mother's passing.

"That's easy to find," the young man says and he explains how to get there. "If you want a ride, you can have one," he adds. "My dad's coming for me."

"I don't need a ride."

"Let us take you," the young man insists. But Rodney shakes his head no and walks off.

He likes to stroll along city streets when they're empty. And he's only thirty-seven, his legs are strong and elastic, more than capable of moving from place to place on their own power.

**A** few nurses are chatting at a kiosk when Rodney walks in. One of them says she can take him to where his mother's body is being held. The nursing home looked like a warehouse to Rodney when he approached it, but there was a sign in front that told him it was the right place.

The nurse talks as she shepherds Rodney down long white hallways. "Your mom had good friends here," she says. She's a big woman, the nurse, in her early thirties. There's a door every eight feet or so, most of them closed, pumping sounds working inside, but occasionally a door is left open, the room beyond it silent and empty, the equipment unplugged.

"Her body was moved to our chapel. The old-timers get nervous for a few days after one of them passes. You understand."

She continues to gabber. Rodney smiles if she tries to reassure him or nods thoughtfully if she's describing something that sounds technical. Rodney doesn't pay attention to her. He thinks about his mother. It's been five years since he saw her last. Even before then, when he was away in the army, Rodney didn't see her all that often, and that was fine by him. He prefers a quiet, lonesome kind of life. It's no great stretch to say that. The bustle and prying of family makes him nervous. His mother's parents didn't like coming to Omaha when they were alive, them the only other people he knew from Hastings, and they insisted on meeting at a restaurant outside the city when they visited, near the suburban hotel they stayed in. They were all embarrassed, having to do it like that. Being around family is a big embarrassment for everyone. Rodney understands this.

When he and the night nurse get to the chapel, Rodney is surprised to find that most of the chairs are filled with residents, ten to fifteen of them. The old folks face the casket, but they turn to look at Rodney as he nears the room, waiting to see if he'll enter or walk past.

"Who are they?" Rodney asks.

"We hold a vigil when one of them dies," the nurse explains. She shows Rodney to an empty seat and settles in next to him. "It helps. These people will miss your mother. Some of her friends." Then she whispers, "A few of them just like to come and sit. Busybodies. You understand."

The chapel is bright, spotlessly clean, and beside the chairs there's a bier draped with blankets on which the casket rests. A Chicana nurse sits beside the door and wears a pink smock and a white cap that tilts atop her hair. At the front, one of the old ladies cries, a large woman in a loose dress who leans against the casket, her chair pulled close. It's a strange thing to Rodney, this woman's weeping, because none of the other residents cry with her. He wants her to stop carrying on and gets the feeling that the rest of the people in the room do too.

"I'll leave you to your thoughts," the nurse who brought him says. "If you need anything, I'll be at the kiosk. The funeral is tomorrow morning. That's today, I guess. In five hours or so, when the pastor gets here. That gives you some time with the coffin, as you'll want to do." And then, "I hope you knew a pastor was coming. It was her wish to receive final rites."

"Of course," Rodney says.

"The lid is closed, but we can open it. I'll do that," the nurse says, standing up, "so you can see her."

She starts toward the casket but Rodney stops her. She halts and looks at the blotch on her arm where he touched her. "You don't want me to?"

"No," Rodney says.

"You don't want to see her one last time?"

They stare at each other for a moment, Rodney and the nurse from the kiosk, both of them embarrassed as the old folks murmur about what's happening.

"I understand," the nurse says, although it's clear she doesn't. She leaves the room without saying another word.

**N**o one speaks in the chapel. They slump in the chairs, stare at the crucifix on the wall or down at their slippers, or play with something in the pockets of their robes, or readjust a walking stick if one lies across their lap. Most of the residents are in pajamas and Rodney wonders if they've been here all night. It's nearly four a.m., he notices, looking at a clock on the wall.

He closes his eyes after a while but catches himself before he nods off. He doesn't want to fall asleep in this room, with these people, and for a while his nerves keep him awake. The residents look at Rodney then nod to each other. They know who he is. One of the old men along the wall rests his chin on his hands, clasped over the end of his cane, and stares hard at Rodney, at the sun-baked surface of Rodney's face, at his hands crooked and shaky from holding the vibrating controls of heavy machinery for what feels like many years. They eye Rodney, like they're here for the sole purpose of sitting in judgment of him, this son of a woman who's passed. All the while, the woman at the front weeps, quiet yet persistent. None of the others move to comfort her. It's this that makes Rodney think they're here just to see him, to see what he looks like, to bear witness to his being here. If any of them would offer condolences to the crying woman he'd feel different about it, or if they shed tears themselves or lay hands on the pine casket. Sitting in the chapel, having these old folks watch him, it makes him feel like he too is dying, or that he should be.

Another of the women leans over eventually and says something into the crying woman's ear. It doesn't make a difference, she still weeps. The nurse tells Rodney that the crying woman was his mother's friend. "Very devoted," she says. "Her only friend in the world."

Over the next two hours the residents nod off, wake up a few minutes later, then go to their rooms in clusters of two or three. Even the nurse in the pink smock leaves, her shift over, so that by sunrise it's only the old lady at the front and Rodney stiff in his chair at the back. The old lady has quit weeping and sits farther away from the casket, blotting her face with a tissue.

An administrator comes into the room soon after the shift change and sits next to Rodney. "You're the son?" she asks, resting her hand on the seat next to his. "I want to let you know that the pastor has called and she'll be here in an hour or so. That's when the service will begin and there's no stopping it then. Nurse Haskell told me about last night. If you want to have a final glimpse of your mother, now's the time."

All Rodney says is, "No." He's silent until the administrator excuses herself.

It isn't until then that the old woman at the front rises and walks to Rodney. She moves haltingly, rests her droopy weight on an aluminum walker. A paling redhead, her thin hair hangs loose over her ears, a few strands still in curls.

"I tend not to need this," she says, indicating the walker, "but it's a long night to be here for these vigils."

"You're my mother's friend." Rodney's voice cracks, this the first real thing he's said in hours. "The nurse told me you were."

The old woman closes her eyes and smiles when Rodney says this, her red face creasing, becoming even redder.

"Come with me, Rodney," the woman says. A twinge of a brogue sneaks out when she says his name. "Follow me."

She takes Rodney to her room so he can wash his face in the sink of her bathroom. She gives him a towel and a fresh bar of soap, then closes the door behind him. Rodney lingers a long time in the bathroom, running cold water over his hands, examining the chair in her shower as he stands at the sink. When he's finished she's leaned against the doorframe without her walker. She's crying again and waiting to embrace him. Her body engulfs his skinny limbs. He kind of lifts under her arms as he hugs her because he's taller and stronger. It's strange to him how he lingers to comfort her. Rodney feels a surge of contentment rush through his body, holding this old woman.

"There," she says. She touches his face, still damp with lather at his sideburns. "Now you look presentable."

They sit together at the front of the chapel as the pastor performs the rites then Rodney allows the old woman to stand at his elbow during the burial at a cemetery outside of town. They are the only two at the plot, besides the pastor and the gravedigger, to witness the patter of soil falling on his mother's wooden box, bits of white root showing in the dirt. When the pastor takes them back to the home the old woman asks Rodney if he would like to come to her room and rest a while. "If you have nowhere else to be," she says, "you're welcome to stay."

"I took the train," Rodney explains. He remembers that his return doesn't leave until nearly three a.m. His plans are vague, at this point of the day, as to how he will pass the more than fourteen hours before the train takes him back to Omaha. It occurs to him that he might not be welcome here, if he tries catching a nap in the park, if he wanders too close to an elementary school playground. He doesn't know what the cops are like in Hastings, if they will judge him at first sight like the old folks at the vigil had, or if they will leave him alone like the police at home often do. Being here without anything to do could mean trouble for a man like him.

When the old woman asks again if he'll stay with her for the rest of the day, when she says that there's coffee in her room, Rodney feels lucky to have found her.

He wakes up later after napping in a chair beside the old woman's bed. She gives him the TV remote and tells him to watch what he wants. A Cubs' matinee is on. He doesn't care much for the Cubs, but bad baseball is better than none.

Rodney gets comfortable in the room after a while, talking to the old woman between pitches. It makes him feel like a nice person. Even though he never came to visit his mother, he's not a bad man. He didn't deserve the looks those old folks gave him, how the pastor locked her car the instant Rodney closed the door after himself. Rodney was used to these things, whether he deserved them or not. And his never coming to visit, that's just the way he was with his mother. If she ever felt differently about their arrangement she never said anything to him.

She was middle-aged when Rodney was born, his mother, accustomed to privacy and calmness. She didn't like doing for other people what they could do for themselves. There was no waiting on hand and foot to serve the men in her house, so Rodney knew the value of keeping quiet and taking care of his own business. But it wouldn't be fair to say that things were bad with his mother, like the cold stares at the vigil implied. It had been five years since he'd seen her, but Rodney loved his mother, that's safe to say, as much as he's loved anything.

The old woman understands this, Rodney thinks, because she loved his mother too.

After there's the singing for the seventh-inning stretch, the old woman opens a drawer and pulls out a store-bought cake under a plastic dome. She takes the cake, German chocolate, with both hands and gives it to Rodney, then shuffles back to the drawer for a spatula, a paper plate, a plastic fork, all of which looks like it's been lifted from the cafeteria.

"Please stay off the bed," the old woman says, "while you're eating."

"They let you run out for cake?" Rodney asks.

"They'll take us to the store if we ask. There's a shuttle van."

"I guess that's right." Rodney remembers seeing those vans around the city before, old folks in the back. He stands from the bed with the plastic dome and moves to the chair.

Rodney cuts himself a piece of cake as the old woman tells about herself, how her kids, the ones who are still alive, are wicked like their father was. "They wish I was dead. I don't mind knowing that. I turn a hundred this winter." She nods her head to confirm it. "It isn't like I planned on living this long."

The old woman says she moved here from Ireland, a long time ago, because her brother claimed there was a man in America who would marry her. "It was a load of bunk. There was a man looking to marry, but he wasn't like Tom said." She tells Rodney how everyone in her family insisted she was an ugly girl and should be happy to have a husband at all, even if he did mistreat her. Her husband died forty years ago, so it worked out in the end.

"Tell me about yourself," the old woman says. "Your mother never said much." Rodney sits up in his chair and looks at the old woman. "Tell me," she says. "What do you do for a living?"

Rodney looks back at the television for a time, pretending to watch the game. "I'd rather not tell you," he says.

"Don't worry. There isn't much that surprises me anymore, if it makes you feel better to know that."

"I don't bother no one," he says. "I live alone."

Rodney watches the old women pop the plastic dome back on the cake and set it near his jacket so he'll take it home. He senses the warm feeling surge through him again as he watches her fuss over cleaning the spatula and the plastic fork.

It's then that Rodney tells the old woman he's a gospel singer.

"Is that right?" she asks, her voice rising with surprise. "A singer?"

"Yes, ma'am," Rodney mutters. "It's for a bunch of churches in Omaha. I do the solos."

"I don't believe it," the woman says.

Rodney flinches, half-smiling to cover his nerves. "It's true," he says.

"Did your mother know?"

Rodney hesitates and looks to the ceiling, his shoulders dropping. "I couldn't say. We didn't talk about it. Not about work. She did love to hear me sing, I know that."

"She never mentioned it to me," the old woman says. For a long time she looks at Rodney, her head crooked, staring at his mouth, his neck, as if imaging what he'd look like standing at the front of a church straining to belt out some high-arcing gospel. "Would you sing for me?" she asks.

"Now?"

"You could sing a hymn. What do you know?" she asks, pinching a strand of hair out of her eyes. "Have you ever sung 'All is Well with My Soul'? Of course you have, that's a standard."

Rodney pauses, looks back at the TV. "I'm not sure," he says.

"Well, don't you know that one?"

Rodney nods his head—and it's true, he knows the hymn. That was one thing his mother always liked to do. On Sundays, even if they didn't go to church, they would sit in the front room at the piano and sing. Rodney learned many hymns this way, his hand on his mother's back as she sat at the piano to play the accompaniment.

"Well, if you know it." The old woman touches his arm with her long fingers. "Will wonders never cease," she says. "A gospel singer."

Rodney looks away from her before he starts singing the hymn. It's the warm feeling that makes him think he can do it —even though it's been a long time since he's tried to sing— and because the old woman asked him to.

His voice croaks when he begins, falling into a lower register, and then higher, unable to find or hold a note, until he stops to clear his throat.

"Try again," the woman says. She closes the door then returns to the edge of the bed.

"*When peace flows like a river, attending my way. When sorrows like the ocean roil below. I will say to my Lord, it is well.*"

Rodney thinks he remembers the hymn, the lyrics are mostly right, but his voice falters again. His tone is off, flat then sharp, then he's not really singing at all, but only humming the tune to himself, a word popping out now and then, until his noise peters off. He stares at the corner of the room, his whole body trembling to keep from letting out his regret.

Rodney hears the old woman. She's weeping. Rodney looks and sees her eyes water.

"I'm sorry I made you cry," he says. "This was the wrong thing to do."

"No, no. It's a beautiful hymn!"

Rodney moves to the woman and puts a hand on her back. "I shouldn't have said anything about being a singer."

"It was beautiful," the old woman repeats. She shudders when Rodney embraces her, they both do, his arms under hers again, his face on her shoulder.

"I'm glad you sung it. You've done all right."

**I**t's six a.m. when his train pulls into Omaha. As he walks to the Kellogg Rooming House, the plastic bubble with the cake held in front, Rodney thinks about how he'll never see the old woman again. It doesn't upset him that he lied to her about being a gospel singer. He wanted to make her feel better. It was his mother's funeral, after all, the funeral of this old woman's best friend.

His room looks empty when he gets back to the Kellogg, but this doesn't bother him either. Rodney takes off the green suit and returns it to its spot in his closet. He stands there in his underwear for a little while then puts on his work pants, changes his undershirt, lies gently on the bed with his hands behind his head as he looks out the window.

There wasn't much time to grab his things from his girl's house this last time they broke up, before she came back from her job. Her brother stood in the living room watching him.

"C'mon, man. You know I won't take nothing isn't mine."

"I know it," his girl's brother said, arms crossed over his chest. "But she asked me to. She said to stand here and supervise, so that's what I got to do. She's my baby sister."

"You don't have to do nothing you don't want to," Rodney said. He kicked a box across the floor but regretted doing it. It wasn't her brother's fault that he had to watch. Things just hadn't worked out between Rodney and his girl, that was the problem.

Most all he has now are clothes and most of them are ratty. Olive work pants the city gives him, a bunch of tee shirts. Rodney mows grass in parks and vacant lots, around abandoned houses. He has a hot plate in his room, on a table next to his bed because he likes to cook lying down. There's a pine closet that sticks out from the wall by the door and his bed is angled so he can look out the window. His girl had a TV and she paid for cable. Rodney kind of misses watching what was on each night, most of all in the summer after mowing was finished. He misses lying on the couch with his girl too, even though he won't let himself miss her. Most of the time it's more comfortable to be alone, that's how he sees it. Rodney's legs are hot and he doesn't like being shut up in a room with somebody else whose legs might also be hot. They'd make things worse for each other.

His room at the Kellogg has a big window, which is what he watches after work now, the downtown buildings reflecting the last light of sunset. And then the fluorescent lights of the offices pop on after a while. It's a drowsy happiness this gives him.

In the morning he sits outside on the edge of a flower box and waits to be picked up and taken to where he will work for the day. Rodney has mowed for the city a long time, fifteen years or more. The man Rodney works with has learned a lot about him over the years, but even he doesn't know Rodney's mother was a white lady, that she came from Hastings and moved east to work for Mutual of Omaha in the fifties. She held more than a few jobs for them, over three decades, all clerical, before there were computers on every desk. Rodney's father worked at Mutual too, that's how they met. He was a custodian. They lived together for a few years in the Leavenworth neighborhood. It wasn't such a great place to live, just as the Kellogg isn't now, because there were junkies on the sidewalks and slumlords let most of the houses go to shit. But the people who lived there would let you be. They wouldn't hassle you for doing things differently than most folks wanted you to. Rodney knew this. He understood.

His father left when Rodney was thirteen years old, but he came back to visit most weekends, even when his life was running short, living alone by then in some innavigable parcel of land north of Cuming, south of Ames, east of 40th, west of the river. The man died and was buried during the three years Rodney was away in the army. Rodney could have had a furlough to return for the funeral, if he'd requested one, but he didn't. His mother had moved back to Hastings by that time too, since Rodney was in the military and she'd retired early. She was fifteen years older than Rodney's father. She worked a long time even after she retired from Mutual, simple stuff she was used to doing with insurance forms, for a while at the hospital in Hastings, a few years after that for a shyster lawyer.

Rodney wished someone would have been there to meet him when he came back from the army, but it wasn't a big deal. In those days men had to drive up from base after serving, which was from Arkansas in his case. He rode with a few guys he knew who were heading his way, another from Omaha and a couple from Sioux City who had the car. They stopped at the dog track in Council Bluffs because the two with the car wanted to gamble.

The family of the other guy from Omaha was waiting outside. That guy wanted to give Rodney a ride. "C'mon, buddy. Get in the car," he said, but Rodney shook his head and jogged after the two from Sioux City who were entering the track. "I'll find a ride," Rodney yelled back. "I'm going to bet some."

Rodney did like to watch the greyhounds run. That's what he did for a few hours, even after the guys with the car decided to head on. He sat inside the smoke-dense building with a smattering of other men who bent over their laps to study the odds. Rodney distracted himself by watching the greyhounds pound the earth on the other side of the glass, those long dogs chasing a mechanical rabbit along the rail. They went around the track and then back into a box.

He hadn't thought about it in real terms until then, that his father was dead. It made him sad that his dad died young—he didn't even know what had done it. Rodney wondered if he was a man then, since he no longer had a father. If that's what would do it.

During an intermission he walked outside and across the parking lot, jumped a fence near the interstate and jogged across the bridge to Omaha. He was in fatigues still, a rucksack sagged over his shoulder. Rodney couldn't keep his breath running over the bridge and had to stop every so often to look down at the river, as if he were lost in a strange country, a new man in a lonely and desolate place.

It was that summer Rodney found the job mowing. Then there was the man he worked with to talk to if he wanted. And he'd see his mother a few times each year until she was unable to travel. And then he met his girl, although that never lasted as long as they thought it would.

**R**odney and the other man work this afternoon in an overgrown lot on Park Avenue. This is still his neighborhood, his part of the city. First they roll the mowers off the trailer, then tilt the blade houses up to unwind grocery sacks and wire fencing from the blades, then they put on goggles and gloves, spray bug repellant that smells like bleach on the fabric that covers their legs and arms. Rodney surveys the yard through blustering clouds of mosquitoes, looking for objects that might break the mowers—pieces of metal, chunks of lumber, a broken suitcase—and for bodies that have been dumped.

He's heard stories about corpses hidden in the weeds, girls with skin coal black from decay, their shirts torn off, skirts pulled up over their hips, but he's never come across one.

The address of the house is spray painted in big orange numbers across the front. This house had a fire, a long time ago by the looks of it, and was abandoned. Through a hole in the roof Rodney sees the charred frame of two-by-fours and what looks like an exercise bike missing its wheel, the slow drift of white summer clouds churning in the sky beyond the hole in the roof. Closer to the house there are empty bottles of booze, aerosol cans, containers of isopropyl alcohol meant to jumpstart cars that folks will drink if they're cold enough. Homeless people live here in the winter, in houses like these, leaving behind piss stains and soiled clothes that can't be worn anymore.

After starting the engine, Rodney drives towards a wall of weeds and pushes it over with the mower, then, as he circles the yard, his tires etch a concentric pattern into the undergrowth, jigsawing around the fixtures, a fire hydrant, a light pole. The engine jumps under his seat, straining to turn over as it chops weeds and grass and beer bottles and whatever else is in there, stirring up dust and ten thousand furious insects.

Rodney keeps thinking that he would like to have sung the hymn right for the old woman at the home. He doesn't feel bad about lying, about saying he's a gospel singer, but he would like to have sung to her the way the hymn was meant to be sung. As he kills the engine after mowing up to the foundation, Rodney thinks that maybe one day he will sing to her, or to someone else, to the lowdown woman in the room next to his who caterwauls the blues every night. He used to sing all right and might be able to again. It doesn't make a lot of sense to him, sitting on top of the mower, watching the bugs settle back to the earth, but maybe one day he'll sing again.

Aaron met Tamara Jones outside a liquor store in Omaha. It was just a come-on. She walked out and Aaron took her picture. She laughed at him at first. He charmed her with persistence.

She kept a room in a boarding house and that's where they went to drink. They had some beers and screwed. It wasn't anything special.

Tamara sang along with the albums she played the whole time he was there. She only ever stood up to use the bathroom at the end of the hall, or to flip a record. She laid naked on her bed and wailed disconsolate incantations, tilted at different keys, half-notes, trying to exorcise the slow undulations of her blues.

It really bothered Aaron the way she did it.

## Bad Faith

### 1

It was after a show at Sokol Underground. I'd been driving up to Omaha once or twice a week that semester and having a few drinks near the back of the room while the bands played. Nothing serious. Not like some girls. Just a g-and-t or two in that smoky basement venue under the gymnastics club, listening to the bands. I bought their albums, stuck their pins to the strap of my bag then drove back to Lincoln when the show was over.

Things changed when I saw the Zapruder Films. A couple of guys from the band invited themselves over to my friend's place for drinks. She talked me into going too and it wasn't such a big deal. I wasn't seeing anyone at the time. My friend Allie was tall and buxom, a blonde in a skirt and banana-yellow tights, with a blue headband. I was the opposite of her, short, but was trim enough to get noticed. Me and Allie knew each other from high school, back in Aurora, the town we grew up in. The guys from the band were named Sammy and Eric, and they both played guitar. They'd known each other a long time too, had met in junior high homeroom and started listening to the Ramones. "The rest is history," Sammy told me, though I hadn't asked him about it. Their band wasn't well-known. I'd never heard of them anyway. They weren't very good and were just opening for Malkmus because their drummer was the kid brother of a guy who used to play bass for Pavement. Something like that. I wasn't really listening.

The four of us watched *Fargo* and drank screwdrivers in Allie's apartment. There weren't enough glasses to go around so Sammy drank his out of a cereal bowl. Monopoly was pulled out of its box but we didn't end up playing. It was too much trouble to count out money. We just watched the movie and laughed about each other's accents. The Zapruder Films were out of Boston. They drawled in ways different than we did.

Then Allie and Eric kissed for a while, rubbing each other's jeans while Sammy and I sat on the couch across from them, pretending we didn't see what was happening, like we were very interested in the movie. I think of this whenever I see William H. Macy on TV now—how I sat like a mouse next to Sammy while Allie got on his friend.

Allie took Eric to her room. She grinned wildly at me as she closed the door, leaving me alone with Sammy.

"Don't worry," he said. "I have a girlfriend, but there's an agreement in place."

I said, "Oh." I didn't really understand what he was saying.

"I'm not supposed to do anything below the waist," he explained. "Otherwise we're good. She understands what goes on out here."

I hadn't wanted to do anything with Sammy, but when we started kissing it wasn't such a big deal. It was sexy the way his tour scruff scratched my lips and how the calluses on his fret hand tickled the skin of my neck. His long curly hair and days'-old clothes were permeated with cologne and sweat, cigarette smoke. It was cliché, I knew this, and it caused me to vacate my senses.

Sammy pulled my shirt off and teased me in ways no one had before. With the guys at the dorm it was more like they were tuning a radio, but Sammy knew what he was doing. He somehow knew my body.

I wanted to draw the line somewhere, to stop him before he went below my waist—like his girlfriend had made him promise—but I couldn't overcome the fluency of his experience. He pulled off my tights and panties so he could go down on me. But before I'd even felt his tongue, he changed course and was on top, working around my fingers to push his thing inside.

"Don't," I said. But he insisted. Maybe he was egged on by my objection, by the fact that, even though I was wet, he had difficultly working his way in.

I tried to stop it from happening, by constricting my muscles, by clenching myself tight, but I was slick and his member designed for this action, long and sleek. It still burned as he wormed inside, and in those few minutes he held out before coming on my stomach. Allie and Eric, I learned later, watched from her bedroom door. She told him I was a virgin and they joked about that as Sammy humped.

The part I felt bad about was how I betrayed myself by getting wet. I tried to explain to Sammy how I hadn't wanted to do it, once it was done.

"Why were you wet then?" He laughed in that spiteful, mocking way guys do when they think we're being stupid. "Don't lie," he said. "You were wet. That means you wanted to. Everyone knows that."

After Sammy turned his back to me and fell asleep, I convinced myself that what happened didn't count as my first time because I hadn't wanted him to do it. It was like an examination, asexual, unloving, and nothing more. I fell asleep then too, believing this.

It wasn't until the next morning that I regained my senses, in the kitchen at breakfast with Allie and the two guys from the band. My dress was stretched and hung loose from my body, my legs bare and shoeless, my tights and sandals stuffed in my purse.

Allie's impish face told me more than I wanted to know. She was giddy for me. And from the way Sammy grimaced as I sat across from him, avoiding eye contact, I knew that I'd come to a breaking point with my old life. I couldn't say anything to him. He'd changed me and everyone knew it.

It was after breakfast, with the Zapruder Films on the road again, that I told Allie what happened.

"We were watching," she confessed. "That's pretty much how it's supposed to go. Don't turn yourself into a victim."

On the drive back from Omaha I decided to leave school. My father came to rescue me after I called and asked him to. He helped load my things out of the dorm into his Park Avenue. It would have been too embarrassing to have him watch me pack, to have my Amazon roommate edge by in nothing but a towel like she'd done on move-in day, her hair dripping wet from the showers, my father's forehead flushed and sweaty. So I packed first and waited by the dorm lobby door. I leaned against the radiator and searched for his Buick, my face pressed against a freezing pane of glass until the tip of my nose ached. When I ran to his car I could feel the hot spots on the back of my jeans where the metal of the radiator had touched my legs.

## 2

Chadron Gutschow steadies himself at the top of a ladder. He unscrews a burnt-out light bulb then drops it into a plastic sack. Alex hands him a different bulb from another sack and Chadron winces when the bare bulb he's screwing in illuminates. He says, "It's going to be a long weekend," and laughs with his roommates as he rubs his eyes.

The doorbell interrupts them, Chadron on the ladder. Jeff opens the door to reveal Chadron's wife Amy on the other side. The men stare at her for a moment, they grin dumb. Amy wears jeans tucked into snow boots and a puffy black coat. This house belongs to her and Chadron, it's her name on the deed, in fact, but she's been gone eight months, in the Twin Cities, and has in many ways given up claim to this house. Even so, she looks pissed to see these two men standing in her living room, her husband out of sight.

"Where are you, Chadron?"

"Up here," he says, humped over the top of the ladder. He's a tall man. His hair self-cut with scissors, choppy and short.

Jeff closes the door after Amy comes inside and follows behind her. Chadron climbs down and then the three men circle her, their proximity somewhat accidental. Chadron worries how Amy sees them, as she looks them over. He and his roommates all look similar, the rough haircut, their uniforms from the animal testing facility—green tee shirts, off-brand dungarees, velcro tennies. At the plant, it's their job to exercise the subjects at a fenced-in area they call the Dog Shit Factory.

This is the Friday before Christmas, so Jeff says they should celebrate. He goes to the kitchen to dig in a cabinet. "The first round is on me," he laughs, cracking the seal on a bottle of Kessler while Alex pops ice cubes into glasses at the sink.

Chadron waits for Amy to say something. The two of them alone in the living room. There's different furniture now, polyester sofas from the Salvation Army, a wooden chair that sits in the corner. Since she paid for it, Amy took their furniture with her to Minnesota when she left.

"You came back," Chadron says, holding his hand out to shake hers. Tears build in his eyes.

"I won't stay long." Amy walks past Chadron to the kitchen. "Just in town to visit my folks," she says. "And to take care of some business."

In the kitchen she sits with Alex and Jeff. Jeff leans into the table and drips tobacco spit into a Gatorade bottle. An odor of wintergreen fills the house while Chadron watches them from the living room.

"Only two bulbs this time," Alex says, looking at the ceiling. He has a dark complexion. People in high school wondered if he was a gypsy. "This is Jeff," he says to Amy. "I'm Alex."

"Get in here," Amy says to Chadron, pointing to the empty seat. After he sits, there's a drink in front of each of them.

"Don't forget to throw in." Jeff looks at Amy while he taps the brown plastic Kessler bottle. "We all chip in for booze."

"Shut up," Alex whispers. "She don't need to pay."

"This is her house," Chadron says.

"Yeah," Jeff whispers back, "but we're the ones paying rent."

The window next to the table is dark and all the lights in the house are on because it's easier than fiddling with them if they change rooms. Later, they'll move to the sofa and watch TV. It's what most men in the world do when they lack an essential ingredient—talent or ambition—they sit around a dreary room and drink.

"I meant to call you this week," Chadron says. "It's been two weeks. That's the longest I've ever gone."

"It's been a month," Amy says. She wears her coat zipped under her chin.

"I call you regular," Chadron says. "This month's an exception." He adds, "We been real busy at work." The other two laugh at him. "Last night I was going to call. But we got some Glenlivet."

"It wasn't really Glenlivet, Shaddy." Jeff frowns as he says this, the edge of his mouth pulling down the droopy skin of his babyface. "I found the bottle in a closet and filled it with Kessler."

Chadron allows his smile to fade as he looks to his wife. He can't say the right thing.

"Let's go outside," Amy says, looking at Chadron. She wrings the fingers of one hand with the palm of the other. "I need to talk to you."

When they're outside Chadron asks Amy what the problem is. From inside he can hear the TV pop on, the other two calling spots on the sofa. "I told you they were living here," he says.

"I know that." Amy pulls a green hat over her hair, earlobes sticking out the bottom. "They're real pieces of work."

"We didn't make a lease or nothing. I can ask them to leave."

"That isn't necessary."

He looks up at the house, standing on the porch. It was a wedding present from her parents, a bungalow with white vinyl siding. There's a chimney on the roof that pumps out steaming exhaust from the furnace and through the curtainless windows Chadron sees Alex and Jeff on the sofa watching TV, their guts stuck out as they sip Kessler.

"Will you please get in the car?" Amy is across the lawn, next to the Neon.

"What's that?" Chadron asks. "Where are we going?"

"Get in the car."

"I'm coming." He hurries down the walk and slides into the passenger side. "Don't you want me to drive?"

"No. You've been drinking."

"But, Amy. So have you."

"Put your seatbelt on," she says. "You're not going to drive my car."

Days later, Chadron will remember that it was his wife who told him to get in the car. It was her idea from the beginning.

**C**hadron and his roommates had eaten an early Christmas dinner in the basement of the Unified Presbyterian Church earlier that week. The UPC Men's Club organizes meals on Thanksgiving, Christmas, and Easter. In December it's honey baked ham, beans, scalloped potatoes, white bread, mincemeat pie. The year prior a farmer shot them a goose.

Some parishioner on the serving line handed Chadron a loaded tray and pointed to where Alex and Jeff had already settled at a card table near the exit. The three of them wore their uniforms from the Dog Shit Factory, having seen to the mutts that morning on their way to the church. They smelled earthy and acidic, like the sick animals they played with, and vaguely of the previous night's liquor in their skin. Alex wore a cigarette behind his ear.

Most of those eating were familiar to Chadron, people from AA, some who worked in the feedlots with him, when he worked there. Mistletoe hung from a doorway and the men jokingly pushed each other under it, calling the younger men faggots if they didn't move away quick enough. Chadron and Amy had been to this church for Sunday services before, when they were first married three years ago. These people knew all about him, probably more than he knew himself.

"You call Amy?" Alex asked, stirring his green beans in with the potatoes.

"Yeah, you call her?" Jeff echoed. This was something they each had an interest in—whether Chadron would reconnect with his deed-holding wife, or if they could hold on in her house a while longer without being harassed.

"Not yet," Chadron said. "I meant to. I call her every week."

He tore open a packet of salt and poured half of it over his plate, then Jeff took the packet and poured the remainder on his bread and potatoes.

"What do you see in that woman anyway?" Jeff asked.

"Chadron likes Amy," Alex explained, "because she's a smart woman and mouthy. He's seen these attributes in women, of course, but before Amy, he'd never been asked out on a date by one."

"That's not true," Chadron said.

"It's pretty simple, isn't it?"

"She's too good for him," Jeff answered.

"She isn't that great of a woman, really, but Chadron doesn't know that."

"She's still too good for him. Any woman would be. He knows this."

"That's why he worships the ground she walks on. That's why he follows orders."

"It's not that complicated."

"He knows she's too good for him. That's why he likes her. It's like getting something in exchange for nothing."

"That isn't true," Chadron said. "I love Amy. That's what it is. We love each other."

"Hey," Jeff said. He put his hands up. "Don't shoot the messenger."

Alex and Jeff picked on Chadron a lot. They enjoyed a sense of superiority over most everyone in town because they were from rich Lincolnite families. They'd known each other in college, had lived in the same fraternity, and were expelled for ethics violations related to a cheating scheme they devised as a means of passing calculus. Alex was Pre-Med when they were expelled, he'd wanted to be a psychiatrist; Jeff was Pre-Law. They were too smart to work at the Dog Shit Factory—they let anyone who'd listen know this—and were only there because it was an easy paycheck. For some reason they acted like this was a temporary state of affairs, that it was only a matter of time before they transformed into *Dr. Alex* and *Jeff, Attorney-at-Law*. Even Chadron understood those ships had sailed.

"Look alive," Jeff said. "Here comes the clergy." He inched his chair closer to the table and hunched his shoulders over himself.

"Shit," Alex said. "No such thing as a free meal."

"Afternoon, gentlemen." The pastor sat at an open folding chair at their table. He was jowly and had a potbelly that stretched the fabric of his sweater. Amy's father was old friends with the pastor. He was the one who'd helped Amy find work in St. Paul. "I trust this meal is serving you," he said.

"Yes, sir."

"Yes, sir."

"Glad to hear it."

"This is good food," Chadron said, holding up a slice of bread to prove it.

"Good, good," the pastor said. "I'm glad you're enjoying what we've provided."

He put his hand on Chadron's shoulder. "There's no delicate way to say this," he began. "I probably shouldn't say anything."

"What is it, sir?" Jeff asked.

"Well," the pastor said. "Chadron, I was down at the café yesterday and noticed Amy is in town."

"Is that right?" Alex asked.

"That's news to us," Jeff said.

"Now, Chadron. Do what you will. Just thought you would want to know. Not that it's my business—"

"Thank you, sir," Chadron interrupted. "I appreciate it."

"I didn't speak to her personally, but—"

"He understands, sir," Jeff said, winking at the pastor. "We didn't hear it from you."

"That's not what I mean." The pastor lowered his voice. "She mentioned that she isn't coming back—that her intention is to move permanently to Minnesota."

"That a fact?" Alex said.

"It is," the pastor confirmed. He clapped Chadron on the shoulder as he stood. "Just thought you would want to know, there's some papers she wants you to sign."

**C**hadron lies in the back when they've finished. Her coat draped over his naked legs. Amy sits in the front seat, her clothes back on, applying lipstick in the mirror. She pulls a folder from her bag and sets it on the seat. "Put your pants on," she says. They're parked on an access road north of town, between an irrigation pump and some railroad tracks.

"I haven't been with a woman since you left," Chadron says. After a moment, he asks, "Do you still want me to sign?"

"Put your pants on," Amy repeats. She kills the ignition then pumps the clutch with her leg and wiggles the stick into first gear. "We'll go for a walk first."

Chadron and Amy follow the tracks for a good while. It's a cool night but not bad for December. "Compared to Minnesota," Amy says, "this is nice." The fields nearby are plowed under, black clods of soil stretch for miles in every direction. This is a spot they've been to many times, mostly in the days before their love went public.

Chadron moved to Aurora in order to apprentice as a machinist at the Goertzen plant, but it didn't pan out. Young and strong, just out of high school, he was better suited to work stock and ended up at the feedlot, where Amy had a job in the office. She was a few years older than Chadron, she'd just quit college a couple years short of a degree. Her father managed the office, that's why she took the job. It was never her intention to move back to Aurora, she just needed a steady paycheck. "You don't seem like such a shithead," she told him when they first met, standing in the doorway of the dusty, wood-paneled office. "Give me time," Chadron laughed. "I'll prove you wrong."

He doesn't like to talk about it, but the county Chadron comes from is one of the poorest in the nation. The Gutschows lived near the bottom of a rocky canyon, where biker gangs put up shanties to cook meth. Families like Chadron's lived in these places too. There were wildfires there in the summer, and when brush burned, smoke became trapped between the canyon walls and saturated everything with its odor. The kids at school called Chadron Bacon Boy because he smelled like smoked meat.

Chadron was the bright spot of his family, though, because he was physically able, he could move and lift things, he'd finished high school. When he left after graduation, his family stood at the door and watched him load a few boxes and a suitcase into his Pontiac. His parents smiled on him when he turned the engine over, waved good-bye. His three younger brothers and his sister were sitting in the yard. Chadron revved the car's motor before putting it in gear, because it always made the little ones cheer. This time was no different, even though he was moving on.

While they were dating Amy often told Chadron that she was just waiting for someone better to come along, that's why she stayed with him. Chadron laughed when she said this, but he always kind of suspected it was true. It occurred to him a woman will latch on to someone who's bad for her and build the guy up so that he seems better than he really is, all for the appearance that she's doing something substantial with her life. This is why Amy agreed to marry him, Chadron figured. That when she tired of her father saying she was dating a loser, it made a twisted sort of sense that she could prove him wrong by marrying the same guy.

Being with Amy gave Chadron a sense of importance anyway. Their life wasn't so bad then, there were plenty of good times. Chadron made steady money at the feedlot, before Amy left for Minnesota, and he didn't drink too much.

**He** watches Amy survey the fields, the black perimeter of soil, the fence posts that slant out of the ground here and there. "I'd like to take a shot," she says, "if I had a gun. I'd shoot all the time in high school, with some guys off a country road."

"Pumpkins and stuff?"

"Melons mostly."

As they walk down the tracks Chadron tells Amy about a dream he had a few months ago. "Don't let it freak you out," he warns. "It was just a nightmare." Off in the distance, in the direction of the car, a train whistle sounds.

"You were at a nightclub in the city dancing. I wasn't there. The bad part was that you were dancing with this woman. She didn't look like a dyke, the both of you were just having fun, but you let her take you out to her car, and, you two made out, kind of, except, she went down on you too. Your leg kicked in the steamy back window, this lady's face between your thighs."

Amy looks away as Chadron explains. She takes small steps, kicks at the chalky railroad rocks, her hands in the pockets of her coat. She squints when she looks at Chadron, sucking her lips, the moonlight behind her head.

"It was like I was outside the car, watching it. I knew what was happening and it kind of made me sick. Knowing that lady and you were doing those things in the back of a car." Chadron stops and looks at his wife, scratching into his hair. "Does that freak you out?"

"It wasn't a dream," she says, wincing as she shakes her head at him. "I told you about that a few months ago. You called my cell every night then. You were wasted."

"That happened?"

Amy turns her shoulders away from Chadron and walks back toward the car. "There's things you can't understand. Nothing will change that."

He follows her, trotting to catch up. There's litter among the railroad rocks, crushed beer cans and fast-food cups, random pieces of steel. The train whistle sounds again, moving through town.

"Amy," Chadron says, grabbing his wife by the arm. He can see her car in the distance, the train rumbling closer behind it. "You got to come home. I don't want to sign those papers. Things are out of control, but you need to stay with me."

Amy frees her arm and keeps walking. "I'm sorry, Chadron. You know that's not going to happen."

"What do you mean?" Something quivers in his stomach and he feels the tears beginning to well up. He knows that trying to stop them makes it worse.

"You, Shaddy. I'm talking about you."

"This is my fault? You're blaming me?"

"Come on." She pulls him behind her by the hand. "Don't cry."

"You're the one who left me. I'm the one who wants to make this work."

"Nothing is going to change. A woman needs more than drinking Kessler and haunting Aurora. You and those boys can keep renting the house. I don't want to live there."

The ground beneath them shakes before the engine passes. The chug and whoosh of railcars follows. "Here she comes," Amy yells, pointing to the engine lights. Chadron follows a few steps behind her, his face contorted red. She stops to watch the train pass, steel grinding on steel. There are farm implements on open flatbeds and inside the boxcars are tractor tires, fire hoses, bent pipes, other odds and ends, cars with smashed fenders and broken windows.

"There she goes," Amy says. The way she looks at the train, hands clasped over her chest. Chadron doesn't know what to think. She moves past him in the other direction.

Chadron has to jog behind her, his long legs keeping pace with her violent, choppy strides. "What are you doing?" he shouts. She runs faster, leaving him behind, easing close to a railcar until she can grab a service ladder. "I've got it," she shouts, bouncing on one foot until she can pull both up. She stumbles to the flatbed from the top rung and flops to her back. Her arms spread above herself, the puffy black coat heaving. Her breath streams above her in small white clouds that wash away in the train's draft.

"Amy," Chadron shouts. "Wait!"

Amy sits up and looks at him running. She cups her hands around her mouth and shouts, "Jump!"

"What the fuck?" Chadron mumbles, hot all over, taking longer strides to keep up with the train. He notices a break in the path ahead, a wooden bridge that spans a creek and is just wide enough for the train.

He accelerates closer to the car, hands shaking. He reaches for her.

"No," she says. "The ladder."

Chadron stumbling next to the clinking railcar, his chest aching. "Jump," she shouts again. "You can make it."

"I can't!"

Chadron touches the painted metal of the ladder with his fingertips. He lunges for the bottom rung but trips on the rock as he tries to pull himself up. He grasps for the handrail but can't reach.

All he can do is watch, on his chest in the ditch, as Amy bounces away. She stands on the railcar, the moon behind her, and waves her arms in what must be half celebration, half good-bye.

Chadron has no idea where she's headed. It bugs him, later, that neither does she.

## 3

It isn't until the wind cuts through her that Amy actually considers what she's doing. This is December after all and she's riding north on the bed of a railcar after sunset. She nestles into her downy black coat, shoves her hands deep in its pockets, and waits for the train to pass through a town where she can jump into a grassy ditch and roll away from the rails.

She'll have to call her father, wherever she lands, and beg him to pick her up, the way she did in college. A tall man with a dopey mustache, her father would wear gray sweatshirts and blue jeans if he came for her on a weekend, or a tweed jacket and corduroy pants if he had to take time off from work. He never asked why she needed him, but just came for her, then hummed almost happily as they returned home. "My baby girl," he'd say, as if it were part of an old song. "What has happened to you now?"

Amy isn't scared of riding on the train, even if she should be, and she doesn't mind the cold, the way her nose and cheeks burn from it. She's been schooled in patience and won't jump before she has to. She likes listening to the clink and groan of the cars, and smelling the layers of grease that pervade the train.

She lets the first few chances to jump pass her by, hesitating at the edge of the flatcar, and then the next few until several towns are behind her and she's still standing on the precipice, rogue strands of hair working out from under her stocking cap to whip the back of her neck. She stands on the train bed, serves witness to the abandoned industrial yards of small towns, the timber stands and feedlots unmanned during the night.

Eventually she curls against the cargo she's riding with and watches the dark countryside as she rattles into it. Amy is unwilling to jump. She wants to see where this train will take her.

**On** the day her father arrived with the rental van, the day she moved to St. Paul, Chadron just kind of hung out and watched as Amy packed up her half of the house. He laid in bed as she filled cardboard boxes from the grocery store, then he sat on the couch eating cereal and watching baseball, then he stood with his back to the sink, slurping cans of Dr. Pepper until the furniture was loaded out and her clothes boxed up.

"Don't you have anything to tell me," she asked when it was time to leave. Her father had already driven the moving van across town.

"No," Chadron said. "I knew this would happen. The kind of guy I am, the kind of girl you are. We both knew this would happen."

From the moment they first met Amy recognized him as a man she could take care of. She fell for him—sweet, malleable Chadron, her dumb-muscle beau. He adored her with such genuine affection and loyalty, a kind of simple gentility that was lost on most of the men and women Amy's been with both before and since. It was so bizarre to her, the way she acted with him—this just months after dropping out of school in Lincoln—but she was a changed woman, no longer the type who promised things to herself. She took charge and told him the way things were going to be, that she was attracted to him, and what she was going to do with him. He listened, guileless Chadron.

"You know it's *me* who's going to leave *you*," she teased. Sometimes she whispered this to him when he held her too closely, if she felt like he really did love her. Amy knew she was running from something, being with him, and Chadron knew it too.

A friend of her father's found her work in St. Paul, as an assistant in the admissions department of Macalester College. She planned to finish the degree she'd begun at NU. Amy liked the job, but something was still missing. Some vital part of her life was deficient. Her initial months in the Twin Cities were wild, those first loose nights when Amy was let free on the lesser dives of University Avenue, often finding herself in the basement bedroom of some college boy or another, once in the backseat of a car with a woman she met at a dance club, and then there was the man with a red beard from the cigar bar. Even though there was a booster seat in the back of his car, and a wedding band in the ashtray, she still went down on him. Amy never learned the names of these acquaintances. She'd create an alias for the guy then repeat it unprompted throughout the night, refusing to hear his real name. It was a guardedness that nearly masked her melancholy—a mournfulness she transformed into a self-sufficiency of sorts.

These encounters seemed incidental when they happened, forgettable indiscretions. Amy had to reconsider them. Things change, sure, she knew this. Life progresses. It's just that the change you end up with isn't always the one you need. You don't have to accept it. She got to the point where she was an embarrassment to be around for the people who were trying to be her friends. Amy was trashy. That's what happens when you sleep with every guy you know and then hate them afterwards. It's okay to be sad, Amy learned, unless people know you are. Then it's bad for everyone. It's untenable.

These were the reasons why Amy backtracked the weeks before Christmas, to reestablish a hold on herself. She found an apartment close to campus in St. Paul, curtailed her drinking, arranged for part-time admission to the college. With her father's help Amy hired a lawyer to draft papers dissolving her lingering marriage to Chadron and she returned to Aurora for the holiday with the intention of having those papers filed at the Hamilton County Courthouse.

It could have been simpler, but Amy wanted to be with him one more time. She still found Chadron attractive, his rangy muscles, the way his face was always red, partly from sun-damage to his cheeks, partly because of capillaries burst from alcohol, partly from the country bashfulness he couldn't suppress.

Then the train rumbled out from the northern edge of town, blowing by as they pushed against its current. The train's noise was stultifying, its sheer power electrified the very air she breathed. Its surging muscle infused itself in her, compelled her body to move on a parallel circuit. It was almost too easy, the way she pulled herself onto the railcar bed. She wasn't thinking about divorce papers or doing the right thing or how her direction in life had been so long ago untracked. Amy didn't even think about where she might be headed, to where these lines led. It was instinct to attach herself to the rumble, to loose her hair in an astounding wind. Even if the result was painful, she wanted to discover what awaited her at the end of the line.

It's close to morning by the time Amy hops off the train. She has a headache and needs coffee, so she positions herself at the edge of the railcar as it slows into another town, coasting into what looks like half timber yard, half salvage lot. There are long open stacks of lumber. On the other side of the tracks are great mounds of scrap, washers and dryers, the tore-out insides of buildings and wrecked cars ready to be compacted and bound together. Amy hops down, stumbles over rail rock as she lands, her legs shaky from a night of riding ill-spliced rails, then she follows the tracks until she's on the other side of a chain-link fence that edges the rail yard off from the town. The sunlight is orange and yellow in rays that sneak over the horizon, which seems odd to her. The sky usually looks this way only in the evening, or during a storm, when dust rises into a tumultuous atmosphere to color the sky.

Amy realizes that the town is called Valentine by the signs on its businesses. She finds a fisherman's cafe, a small brick building with old men drinking coffee inside. They wear plaid shirts with red suspenders and ball caps with the names of feed companies over the bill. These men resemble her father and his friends from church. Amy orders coffee and sits at a table near the window. The men smell her, she notices, their noses bend in her direction. The odors of the train followed her in, the heavy grease smell, the biting tang of too-fresh winter air that trails those who spent the night outdoors. It doesn't bother Amy if the men stare. She's used to being stared at.

When her coffee is finished Amy decides to call her father. She doesn't really have any other options. The sooner she can get back to Aurora, the sooner she can take care of things and get her car and get back to the Twin Cities. There isn't much waiting for her in Minnesota, but it's what she has now.

**A** skinny man in a tee shirt is waiting to snap a picture of her when she opens the door. There's a flash from his digital camera, and then she sees the man behind it, standing in the street.

"Don't run," he says, hiding the camera at his hip.

Amy stops to look at him, her body twisted in the doorway, confused as to why anyone would take her picture just then.

"Who are you?"

"I noticed you walking across the street," the man explains, circling as he moves closer. "My name's Aaron Kleinhardt. I'm staying at the motel over there." He points to a brown motor lodge down the block.

"I wanted to take your picture," he says. "You're pretty."

"What are you? Crazy?"

"No," Aaron says. "Why would you say that? We don't know each other."

Amy lets the door bang shut behind her, squaring her body to this man. He's a little older than she is, Amy figures, but he dresses like he's trying to look young, in a yellow *Wyoming Cowboys* tee shirt and tight jeans, his feet bare. His hair is stringy and needs trimming. The bangs hang over his eyes and, in order to see, he has to flip them to the side of his forehead. He's friendly, has blue eyes, a big smile that projects his straight rows of teeth.

"Listen," Amy says. She turns away. "I have a call to make."

But she stops, nudges at her scalp where the wool cap makes her hair itch, and stares at him again, this man who's still smiling at her, holding the camera at his side.

"If you don't mind my nerve," Aaron says. He moves gingerly, with pantomime steps over the gravel on the sidewalk. His feet must be freezing.

"I wonder if you'd tell me what you're running from."

"Excuse me?"

"You betrayed yourself." That's how he puts it. "It's the smell, your clothes," he explains. "I've learned a few things about being on the run, believe me, and you have the look of it."

"I have—really?" Amy flusters, turns back to this stranger. "I don't know what you're talking about."

"You don't have to tell me. I see what's going on." He slips the camera into the back pocket of his jeans and takes Amy by the arm, trying to shepherd her across the street.

"Don't touch me," she says, pulling her arm away.

"I'm sorry." He takes an exaggerated step back, palms raised.

"What I wanted to tell you," he continues, "is that you can use my shower if you need to. That's all I wanted to say. If you don't have the money for your own room, you can use mine."

Amy turns and walks away from him as he speaks to her, but again she stops to look back. He's kind of pitiful, the crummy clothes, his scrawny limbs. She laughs to herself at the very image of Aaron Kleinhardt, this pathetic man luring her back to his room.

"How stupid do you think I am?"

"You don't get what I mean," he says, pleased that she's listening. "I'll leave while you're there and wait outside while you shower. If that's what you want."

She can't believe how this man's approached her on the street, in Valentine, or the way his voice fluctuates, like he's constantly defending himself. Amy knows it's a bad idea to stick around, to associate with a man who acts like Aaron acts, but she can't help herself.

**A**aron has her cornered in the room but Amy knows how to handle him. She guides him to the bed and goes to her knees in order to diffuse the situation. She won't lie in the bed with him, not that, but she unzips his jeans and touches the cold damp tip of his prick with her tongue, then takes him into her mouth relentlessly so that it's over quickly and she can get in the shower. He tries to thumb at her crotch after coming but she pushes him away. He won't insist if he's already had his. Amy understands these diversions.

When she emerges from the shower, a long white towel wrapped around her body, Aaron is still on the bed. He's stripped down to his boxers.

"How was it?" he asks, grinning, brushing away the stringy hair that hangs over his eyes.

"Mediocre," she says. "But nice, still, after the night I had."

"Are we talking about the shower?"

It's the way Aaron asks this, a huckster's smirk on his face, and that he'd even ask if giving head was good, that makes Amy feel again that she's made a mistake. She knew this already, when he followed her into the room and wouldn't leave her alone, and then in the moment she capitulated, Amy felt like what she was doing was wrong. But she's been in situations like this before and understands it's a zero-sum game. What can it hurt, that's what she thought. Who will know the difference? If she gets a good shower, it would be worth it.

And she did try calling her father before Aaron convinced her to come to his room, but the call went unanswered. It wasn't her fault if events conspired against her. Standing there on the street, Aaron watching while it became clear that whoever she was calling wasn't going to answer. She couldn't think of another excuse for why she wouldn't use his shower. That is, besides the most obvious, that she didn't like him, that she knew what would happen once they were in his room, that she didn't want to have sex with him.

Amy didn't feel like she could tell Aaron in plain words that she wasn't interested. From the first moment they met she recognized the way he wanted her; she understood it would be easier to satisfy his desires than it would be to avoid them; she didn't have anywhere else to go.

"Listen," she says, freshly resolved to shake him. "Thanks for the shower and everything, but I need to get going."

"Sure." His eyebrows drop. "If you got to leave, I understand."

"It's nothing personal."

"Of course."

"It's not that I didn't enjoy it." They both cringe as she says this, because words like those can only mean their opposite. "You're on your own journey somewhere, I suppose, and I'm on mine. Let's just leave it at that."

Sitting on the bed, hands in his lap, Aaron drops the smile and squints at Amy, as if he's searching for something specific. It creeps her out, standing in a towel while he examines her, even though he isn't looking at her body exactly, her bare shoulders or legs. It's her face he's watching, her hair made curly by the shower steam, the furious glare she feels overtaking her eyes, the way her chin inches back into itself because she's nervous.

It's Aaron who breaks away first, his gaze darting to the door that leads to the street, to her puffy black coat that's hung over the knob.

"You were on a train, weren't you?" The full dopey smile reemerges as his gaze returns to her body. "Not a passenger train, that's not what I mean. They don't run here. I can smell it, the oil, the ozone of dynamos. You hopped a freight."

"I don't know what you're talking about."

"No," he says. "It's okay to admit it. I know about the kinds of things that set folks off into this country up here. I even rode a train like that before. It's a secret, that kind of thing. It's free."

"Okay," Amy says. She leans down to snatch her clothes off the carpet. "I'm leaving."

With the bathroom door locked behind her, Amy dresses quickly. She slips on her jeans as she sits at the edge of the bathtub, then refastens her bra, its wires bent out of shape after sleeping on the railcar. It's when she's holding her shirt that she hears Aaron move, noticing the sound of him walking across the old motel shag, his pressing a hand against the bathroom door. It's dead quiet in the morning. Amy stands stock-still in the bathroom, listening. The door seems to hum, as if Aaron is sliding his fingertips over its surface, his nails imperceptibly scraping the veneer. She jumps when he speaks because she doesn't know what's going to happen.

"Amy," he says, his voice still earnest and unashamed, a hint of begging in it. "If you're going to hop another train, I'd like to come." She stands with her back to the door, a cold shiver running along her spine. She wishes her father had answered when she called him.

"Would you let me go with you?" he asks. Amy hesitates, grips the edge of the sink. "I'm not going to jump a train."

"You can tell me," he says. "I'd like to go on one, if you are."

Their agreement is to jump a southbound.

Amy had left the room, she'd dressed quickly and hurried out the door, slipped around the corner and called her father, misdialing twice because her fingers were shaking. She needed to get out of Valentine and should have kept walking, that was her mistake, because Aaron emerged jogging behind her on the street, wearing only his boxer shorts. He jumped in front of her and Amy had to end the call before anyone answered, cutting off the dial tone as she snapped her phone shut. She stuffed the phone in her pocket because Aaron was standing there, practically naked on this small-town street where they both were strangers.

Somehow he calmed her again and convinced her that they must catch a train together, his voice jumpy trying to make it sound like fun before he rushed upstairs to put his clothes back on. Amy should have run then, but she hadn't. If she was someplace familiar, Aurora or the Twin Cities, or even Lincoln, where there were crowds of people, or folks she knew nearby, Amy would have run from him. But there wasn't anywhere she could go here. What would she tell them, these people that lived in Valentine? That she'd hopped a train and was stuck here? That she went down on this man in a motel room? Nothing had happened that she hadn't allowed to happen. That's what it would look like—that's what they would think—that she was seeking this weird man's attention. She was a stranger too. She couldn't rely on anyone here to save her. So she agreed to hop a southerly, because at least then she would be headed in the direction of Aurora.

When Aaron falls asleep within the first hour it seems like a real blessing, especially when her phone vibrates in her pocket, when Amy sees that Chadron is calling. He's still her husband, she remembers, because they never signed the divorce papers. She left them in her car, then jumped the train and now she's here, wherever this is, somewhere south of Valentine. Amy doesn't answer the call, though, she presses the button on the side that stops the vibrating.

They're passing through another town when Amy notices that her phone is going to run out of battery, and it's this juxtaposition of events that causes her to stand and lean toward the ground rushing by—she's going through a town, her phone will soon die, Aaron's asleep behind her. She nearly jumps. But then she pauses to rationalize with herself.

It seems too simple, that she can jump off the train and walk to town, stop at the library and call her father, that she could escape from Aaron's cloying presence while he's sleeping. And it's while she's thinking these things—remembering the way her father would softly hum, "Oh, Amy, what has happened to you now?"—that she returns the phone to her pocket, sits back inside the boxcar, and decides to hang on a while longer. *This is what I'm doing*, she thinks. She'll wait until they're closer to Aurora before jumping, so she can walk back on her own.

Aaron continues to sleep, curled in a back corner of the near-empty railcar. There's just scrap metal in the car with them, segments of rusty I-beams. *Who is this man?* she thinks again, standing over Aaron as he sleeps, his skinny ankles showing out the bottom of his jeans. He's not particularly attractive, Amy knows this. She's embarrassed that she went down on him, although embarrassed before whom she couldn't say. It doesn't matter. Amy can't think of anyone she's slept with whose looks or personality were cause for bragging.

It's true that Amy hasn't always made her own decisions, she hasn't always been in control of the situations she's found herself in, but, if she could help it, she would never let a man treat her like she's a victim again.

**B**ecause it's just sitting there unattended, Amy digs in Aaron's bag and carries it to the edge of the railcar. Inside she finds his wallet and some other personal junk that isn't interesting, but her fingers jump when she sees his digital camera in the front pocket, wrapped in a small cotton sack. She wants to see who else Aaron has taken pictures of, remembering the way he'd approached her that morning, his obvious ploy to get her in bed.

The first few photos in its history are of Amy herself, a close-up of her face, then one of her leaving the café. She feels something roil in her stomach, before she even realizes what it means, as she finds images of herself walking into the café, and even before then, when she first entered town, long-range shots of her bending over to tie her shoes. It's as if Aaron had anticipated her coming, standing at his motel window with this camera at first light, waiting for a woman to wander into his frame. Amy thought his line was pitiful but she was wrong. These pictures of her coming into town, nearly a dozen of them, showed that he'd planned for her arrival. He'd been waiting to tell her she's pretty.

Amy looks over her shoulder at Aaron, still sleeping, this skinny dweeb who somehow convinced her to go along with him. She wants to hit him, to kick his face in while he sleeps, but she merely closes her eyes, shakes her head in disgust, then turns back to his camera.

There are a few more shots of Valentine and other towns, stone-built town halls and decommissioned tanks in municipal parks, then images of a woman lying naked in bed, covering her face in embarrassment, followed by a few of this same woman standing outside a coffee shop; then a different woman tied-up, her breasts squeezed purple in the cinch of a nylon rope, what happened after Aaron snapped her photo outside a shopping mall; others of a woman blindfolded, her ankles and wrists hogtied, her parts exposed; another of Aaron wielding a knife, biting a woman's nipple as he slices across her belly.

There's a video Amy plays. A big woman lounges in a dark room, the curtains drawn. Her bottom-heavy breasts rest on her stomach as she lies in bed, drinking from a beer can. Her hair is done up in what looks like an old-fashioned style, even though she can't be much older than thirty.

The camera's small speakers distort from the loud music that plays in the room, an undulation of hoary blues music, the big woman singing in chorus between slugs of beer, spread out naked on the bed, her flesh sinking into itself.

Amy turns again to look at Aaron, to see if the video woke him. He's slumped in the corner, arms folded over his chest, sleeping.

His voice is under the music in the video. "*The Kellogg Rooming House. June 15, 2010.*"

The image shakes, as if the camera had been set on a table, although the woman is still the only one on the screen. She's humming to herself, twisting her legs as she lies there, her long brown body full across the bedsheet. There's a pop. The sound feeds back in short crackles. Then two more. The woman in the video drops her beer to the floor. Three small holes appear on her body, two in her stomach and one in her breast. The woman cries, it sounds likes drunk wailing, like she's merely confused and lonely. The video plays for a long time after she's shot, the loud music over her moans as the bedsheet blots red. Long after she stops making noise, stops moving, the video freezes on the image of the woman in her bed, the holes in her stomach and breast.

Amy holds the camera for what seems like a short time. The image of the woman dims and then fades to black. Amy still doesn't jump; even the thought of it has left her. Her head buzzing. Her vision fuzzy outside the borders of the camera viewfinder. She can't control it: Amy thinks of simple

Chadron, her husband back in Aurora, drinking a morning beer at the kitchen table.

Sitting at the edge of the railcar with the camera in her hands, Amy doesn't think that Aaron is awake while she watches the video. She's wrong about that.

The train is going over a bridge. Amy sees this above her through a dizzying matte of tree branches. She's landed at the foot of the pylons that support the bridge. There are whole minutes of blackness and white noise, the sound of train rumble vibrating through bridge feet. Amy feels behind herself. Her fingers bump the blood-sticky hilt of the knife in her back.

She felt the burning of it before she heard Aaron grunt, the knife needling into the softness of her lower back. It was the crescendo of pain rising in her torso that caused Amy to arch away from him, her body going stiff, legs straightening in shock, the fire of the knife at her kidneys. The camera was in her hands, his bag nestled between her legs at the edge of the railcar. It was only by chance that when Amy rolled away the train was going over a bridge that spanned a wide coulee, and that as she fell the thirty feet through snapping tree branches, clutching to his bag, she curled into herself and landed in the spongy gut of a stream bottom.

It's when she bumps against the knife that Amy understands she's still in danger, that the images on Aaron's camera come back to her, and that she's still holding the camera, she still has his bag—and he will come looking for them.

Amy is unable to stand when she first tries. The pain in her back saps the strength from her legs, the muscles battered, but she manages to gain her knees on the second try, and then her left foot as she leans against a tree. She can crutch herself along, grasping from one sapling to another, his bag slung over her shoulder, moving from the spot, down the coulee to where there's light. It's a narrow snatch of forest she's in, a few acres hugging tight to where the railway bridge spans the gully. It gives her enough of a head start on Aaron, though.

He will make sure she's dead, Amy knows this. That's why she drives herself on, advancing quicker as her legs stretch out underneath, the pain in her muscles abating as she moves them. There's still the blooming shock of the knife in her back, where the blade keeps her wound more or less closed, but Amy can't worry about that. She doesn't want to end up like those other women in the camera.

It's when Aaron's bag slips from her shoulder and dumps its contents to the ground that Amy finds his pistol. The bag tilts upside down as it drops, his wallet and notebook fall out, then the gun on top of them. The glint of its plating flashes a ray of light. Amy checks the pistol and sees it's loaded. She secures the safety and stuffs it into her beltline. She unfolds his wallet, removes his driver's license and sees that his name really is Aaron Kleinhardt, just as he told her. If he planned on killing her all along then it couldn't matter if she knew his name.

At the edge of the woods Amy spies the open country of a farm, long furrows of soil ground in by tractor tires during harvest. The trees edge into a straight line where the field begins, along the right-of-way, so she can see a long distance in front of her. Aaron can see too if he's looking. There's an irrigation shed or something like it, a wooden structure in the clearing, about fifty yards away. Amy can just make out its flat roof, its wood shingles worn the same color as the soil. It's getting cold again. As she hobbles across the frozen clods of dirt she can feel the wind blow through her.

She crouches inside the shed once she reaches it. There isn't much to the structure, one main line that humps in and out of a concrete box dug into the ground, a few pipes that sprout near the door with gauges at their ends, the dripping odor of moss. But there's space enough to settle against the wall planks and wait to see if Aaron will find her. She feels behind herself again, touches the sticky hilt of the knife. There isn't much blood. Even with her fall, the blade's channel hasn't widened.

Amy isn't sure what she'll do when he discovers her. She girds herself, holding the pistol between her hands, and whispers that she can do this, she's shot before. And it's true, she's shot a pistol many times. She knows how to prepare the gun, how to stare down the back of it while loading the chamber and how to flip the safety so that it's ready to fire.

It isn't long before Aaron finds her, a few minutes, as if he was poised at the other end of the clearing, watching as she entered the irrigation shed before circling in.

She hesitates, despite herself, when he opens the door, shocked somehow to see him standing there looking pathetic.

"I'm unarmed," he says, holding his hands up by his face, his fingers outstretched. "Please don't shoot."

Amy slides across the concrete floor as far away from him as she can get before jarring the knife against the back wall. She doesn't shoot. She holds the pistol out, both hands squeezed around the gun so that it looks tiny wrapped under her fingers, its barrel emerging darkly from her hands.

"I don't want to kill you," she says.

"Give me the gun, please. You don't know what you saw. There's a good explanation."

Aaron inches closer as he talks, kind of leaning, his feet sliding to catch up. His body becomes bigger in the doorway once he clears it, the flimsy door quivering in the wind behind him, his hands still held out in front.

"Give me the gun and we'll wait for the next train to come."

"Stop moving."

"We both made mistakes today. I'm willing to walk away. Just give me the bag."

Amy feels like closing her eyes, to just black out everything and squeeze until this man is gone. But she holds Aaron in the doorway with her gaze, her jaw stern, eyes flashing a glint of blue above the pistol clutched in her fingers. She sizes him up, determines where she should shoot to wound him, where she can aim to kill. She looks him in the eyes again. It's difficult to look Aaron in the eyes and not falter for an instant, to stifle a flutter of sympathy, because of the way he holds himself. His skinny limbs and bad posture, those ill-fitting clothes made for a younger man. And that half-smile, still he's smirking, like he can't believe that it's come to this. All the while he inches closer.

Amy feels how those other women must have underestimated him, because of the way he looks and acts, like he couldn't possibly get the better of her. But she can see it in his eyes too—in a too-late way like the others—how all this is thrilling him. She knows what's going to happen.

He's started to say something when Amy shoots. She squeezes the pistol until it pops, and then again, hitting him twice in the chest. He still talks, even as he tries to pool blood in his fingers. Invoking the train, trying to sell her. The words end as a sort of gulping. He staggers out of the shed and falls into the dirt.

It's ten minutes or more before Amy is certain he's dead. The gasps of his body twitter out into nothing. Slowly she works to her feet, the burn pulsing from the knife in her back, and then she escapes the shed, the pistol poised in front of her, just in case. She has to step over him, to look down at his pale face still smirking, one eye open and one closed. Amy doesn't falter when she sees his chest bloat. She knows he's dead. It's just the mechanics of his lungs working.

She doesn't cry yet because there's the knife in her back, her clothes wet with blood, and she's walking toward what looks like a farmhouse on the horizon.

Amy fires three shots in the air before she collapses, too weak to continue, using the last of the bullets to attract the attention of the farmer and her husband in the house that's less than a mile away. They're the ones who find her.

## Acknowledgements

My sincerest thanks those who made this book possible. Foremost, to Nicole, for acting in ardent *good faith* to ensure that there's room for writing and literature in this life we've built together; to my daughters, for putting up with a pensive father with aplomb; to my mom for passing on a love for books and never talking me out of fixations; to Karen, for making sure I had time to write most every day, even when there was a baby in the house; and to my family and friends for their support.

I'm grateful for my crew of mentors, advocates, and compatriots: Bill Sedlak, Amber Mulholland, Drew Justice, Ryan Borchers, Stephanie Delman, Jonis Agee, Susan Aizenberg, Bob Churchill, Cleo Croson, Natalie Danford, Nabina Das, Miles Frieden, Amina Gautier, Anne Greene, Jordan Hartt, Arlo Haskell, Nicola Mason, Kassandra Montag, Dave Mullins, Emily Nemens, Amy O'Reilly, Jessica Rogen, Lucas Schwaller, Sam Slaughter, Brent Spencer, Mary Helen Stefaniak, Travis Thieszen, Felicity White, and Mark Wisniewski. A special thanks to Richard Burgin.

Thanks to Queen's Ferry Press, Bradley Cole, Brian Mihok, and Kelsey Hall, for helping get this book to press, and to Erin McKnight for her tireless enthusiasm and guidance.

Finally, this book couldn't have been written without the support of the following organizations: Akademie Schloss Solitude, Key West Literary Seminar, Port Townsend Writers Conference, Wesleyan Writers Conference, Kimmel Harding Nelson Center for the Arts, Creighton University, *Prairie Schooner*, University of Nebraska, 1877 Society and Omaha Public Library.

Photograph by
Travis Thieszen

**Theodore Wheeler** is a reporter who covers civil law and politics in Omaha, where he lives with his wife and two daughters. His fiction has been widely featured in national anthologies and magazines, including *Best New American Voices*, *New Stories from the Midwest*, *The Southern Review*, *The Kenyon Review*, *Boulevard*, and *Five Chapters*. He's been a fellow at Akademie Schloss Solitude in Stuttgart, Germany, a resident of the Kimmel Harding Nelson Center for the Arts, and has won the Marianne Russo Award from the Key West Literary Seminar. He is also the author of a fiction chapbook and *Kings of Broken Things*, a novel that's forthcoming in the spring of 2017.

CPSIA information can be obtained
at www.ICGtesting.com
Printed in the USA
FSOW01n2055130716
22731FS